O9-ABF-303

The 25¢ Miracle

The 25¢ Miracle

by

Theresa Nelson

Bradbury Press New York

Bradbury Press
An Affiliate of Macmillan, Inc.
866 Third Avenue, New York, N.Y. 10022
Collier Macmillan Canada, Inc.
Manufactured in the United States of America
1 2 3 4 5 6 7 8 9 10
The text of this book is set in 12 pt. Simoncini Garamond.
Library of Congress Cataloging-in-Publication Data
Nelson, Theresa, 1948–
The 25 [cent] miracle.
On t.p. "[cent]" appears as the cent symbol.
Summary: Motherless, eleven-year-old Elvira looks for a
mother and finds instead the father she hardly
knew she had.
[1. Fathers and daughters—Fiction] I. Title.
II. Title: Twenty-five [cent] miracle.
PZ7.N4377Ad 1986 [Fic] 85-17061
ISBN 0-02-724370-2

For KEVINS

1

Long before the sun rose on the morning of Elvira Trumbull's eleventh birthday, the smell of rain was in the air. It drifted down the streets of Calder, Texas, hinting at cool, wet breezes blowing somewhere out in the rice fields west of town. It drifted past the Dairy Queen and the Phillips 66 and the Calder High School Stadium, home of the Wildcats, the pride of Chambers County. It drifted on out Interstate 10 and into the Happy Trails Trailer Park, making promises as green and lush as long-ago April. It had been a hard, hot summer for everybody in Calder; it had been even harder and hotter for anybody living in the Happy Trails Trailer Park, where air-conditioning was not necessarily one of the blessings that people counted instead of sheep as they lay sweltering in their beds at night.

The trailer park was tolerated, but not smiled upon, by most of the local citizens. If there had been any tracks in Calder, which there weren't, the Happy Trails would have been located on their wrong side. Not that there was really anything very wrong about the place—or very right, either; it had no personality one way or the other, except for one small detail: a strangulated-looking little rosebush that was fighting for its life in the dirt just outside the door of one of the trailer houses.

This particular trailer was the home of one Henry S. "Hank" Trumbull and his daughter, Elvira, planter of the rosebush and—just now—dreamer of dreams.

"What would you go and do a fool thing like that for?" Hank had shouted angrily, the day Elvira went out for a few groceries and came home with the rosebush instead.

"I don't know, I just d-did," the girl had answered helplessly. She couldn't explain the queer feeling that had come over her when she'd passed the corner where a small, dark, slick-haired man had parked his van and was selling tropical plants in plastic pots and an assortment of rosebushes with their roots bound up in burlap. Her attention had been caught by one bush, somewhat smaller than the others, with yellow blossoms. The red and pink flowers on the other bushes were showier, but there was something about those pale yellow roses that went straight to Elvira's heart and stuck there. Buy me, the yellow rosebush seemed to plead, and Elvira had done it, much to her own surprise and that of the slick-haired man. He had been about to chase her away when she held out the ten-dollar bill that had been wadded up in her fist.

"You want to buy something?" the man had asked.

Elvira had nodded and gestured shyly toward the little plant.

"Ah, you like the Davidica roses, do you? Good choice—excellent choice!" the man had cried, relieving Elvira of her money before she had a chance to change her mind.

Hank had hollered about that rosebush for a whole week, but he hadn't made Elvira take it back. He threatened to at least half a dozen times, but something in his daughter's tremulous silence kept stopping him.

That rosebush had set him to thinking about things, and thinking was something that Hank generally avoided. It hurt too much, ever since Margaret died, anyway . . . In self-defense, he had built fences around those thoughts that troubled him—fences made of Lone Star beer, wrestling matches, and old John Wayne movies playing endlessly on the television.

But something about that rosebush had knocked down those fences and hit him right in his aching, unguarded center. *Think,* Hank Trumbull, the something had ordered. Think about your daughter.

And so he was thinking of her in the small, dark hours of that morning when the smell of rain was slipping into Calder. He was thinking of her, even though he was trying not to, as he sat drinking beer after beer at the counter of the Alamo Lounge, an establishment that was located even farther to the wrong side of town than the trailer park.

Elvira? What was there to think about?

Everything about Elvira made Hank feel uncomfortable and vaguely guilty—the way she had of folding her skinny arms protectively across her flat little chest and disappearing somewhere deep inside herself, of staring at the floor when he asked her a question and stammering when she finally answered, of breathing too loudly through her nose, which was usually clogged up, and wrinkling her forehead so hard when she didn't understand something that, young as she was, there were already the beginnings of two deep furrows between her eyes. *Her* eyes. Margaret's eyes. That was what bothered Hank most of all—those eyes that hungered and thirsted for something that he didn't know how to give—something he had never known how to give, or had forgotten, if he had ever known. Something to do with yellow roses.

"If she'da been a boy, I'da known how to handle her," he said to Shirley, the bartender at the lounge. "Shoot, we coulda done things together—gone huntin', maybe, or fishin', or played a little ball or somethin' . . . But what am I s'posed to do with a girl who never opens her mouth to say boo? Not that there's anything wrong with her brain, acourse," he hastened to add. "She could talk if she wanted to—she's just stubborn, is all—hardheaded as they come. Just like my sister Darla."

"And I don't suppose you're hardheaded at all?" Shirley teased him. He laughed grudgingly and ordered another Lone Star . . .

Darla had been on the edge of Hank's mind all night. She had been after him for the last five years to send Elvira to live with her in Sulphur Springs. A part of Hank told him that she was right. Darla and her husband had money; they'd be able to give Elvira all the things a girl ought to have—pretty clothes and a nice house to live in and whole truckloads of rosebushes, if that was what she wanted. But somehow Hank had never been able to bring himself to give her up. She was all he had . . . But you got to think of the kid, he told himself. You got to think . . . you got to think . . .

He buried his face in his hands.

Margaret had liked yellow roses. The memory stabbed unexpectedly, and Hank pushed it away. No, you don't—you ain't gonna get started again—stay outta my head, Margaret—stay away—leave me alone, will you? Will you just leave me alone?

"You okay, Hank? I think maybe you had eight or nine too many tonight." Shirley laid a hand on the big man's shoulder.

"I'm just fine. Don't start preachin', Shirl—you sound like Darla," he mumbled, getting heavily to his feet and pulling some crumpled bills out of his jeans pocket—the jeans were too tight, but he insisted on wearing them, anyway, as if in punishment for allowing himself to get out of shape. "Time I was gettin' home. You take it easy, now."

"You know it. 'Night, Hank."

Hank laid his money on the counter and walked out into the night. Feels like it wants to rain, he reflected. He was limping a little. He had injured his hip in a high school football game years ago, and it never had healed properly. Any change in the weather was sure to aggravate it . . .

Thunder rumbled darkly in the distance, and Elvira opened her eyes. The smell of rain drifted in through the window screen. Outside, the yellow roses stirred in the rising wind as the first fat drops began to fall.

Rain was falling steadily by the time Elvira climbed out of her bed in the pale morning light. Happy birthday to me, she sang silently to herself, as she stretched and pulled on a pair of shorts and a reasonably clean T-shirt. There was no hint of a celebration in the air—only the stale scent of the cigar that Hank had smoked when he had finally gotten in, a scent that lingered in spite of the rain-washed freshness of the morning.

Elvira was glad it was raining. Maybe the rainwater would perk up her rosebush a little. She pulled her hair back into a ponytail and stared at herself in the mirror that hung over the bathroom sink. Turning eleven had made no great difference in her appearance. She was small for her age, with a kind of blonde fragility about her that might have passed for prettiness if there had been anybody around who knew how to nudge it in that direction. As there wasn't, Elvira was a child to whom few paid the compliment of a second glance.

The sound of Hank's snoring mingled with the retreating thunder. Elvira walked exactly ten steps down the "hall" of the trailer house to the kitchen area. She opened the door of the miniscule pantry and surveyed the territory. Nothing but Wheat Crackles, she noted with disgust. Hank had done all the grocery shopping since the rosebush incident, and Wheat Crackles were a particular favorite of his. Elvira turned on the heat under the teakettle and then poured the cereal into a bowl. Absently, she read on the back of the Wheat Crackles box that Captain Magnificent wanted her to become a member of the "Body-Building-Breakfast-Buddies." (Elvira was a compulsive label-reader. Funny thing about reading, she had reflected more than once—once you learn how to turn it on, seems like there ain't no way to turn it off.) She shifted the box sideways and saw that the Percentage of U.S. Recommended Daily Allowances was still exactly the same as it had been yesterday, and the day before that, and probably even the day before that, although she couldn't swear to Tuesday, since she had eaten cold pizza for breakfast that day. Her eyes traveled on to the fine print at the very bottom:

Guarantee: If you are not satisfied with the quality and/or performance of the Wheat Crackles in this box, send name, address, and reason for dissatisfaction—along with entire box top and price paid—to: General Grains, Inc. Box 1095 Minneapolis, MN 55440. *Your purchase price will be returned.*

Elvira had read that guarantee about a thousand times before, and she had always meant to check it out. Well, today I'll do it, she told herself suddenly. What the heck. It's my birthday.

She finished as much of her cereal as she could stand, poured the rest into the sink, and then sat down again at the tiny kitchen table with a pen and a piece of paper from an old spiral notebook.

Dear General Grains,
I am dissatisfied with the Wheat Crackles in this box. They aren't no good.

Yours truly,
Elvira Trumbull
Happy Trails Trailer Park
P.O. Box 498
Calder, Texas 77597

P.S. They cost me $1.49.

Elvira tore off the boxtop and put it, along with the letter, into an envelope. Just then her father came in, filling the pint-sized kitchen with his bulky form. He sat down at the table. The chair creaked.

"Mornin'," he murmured. His voice sounded hoarser than usual.

"Mornin'," Elvira answered. She noticed that his eyes were redder than usual, too, but she didn't mention it. She knew better than that. "You want some coffee?" she asked instead. "I got the water boilin'."

"That'd be real good," Hank said absently.

Elvira measured the instant coffee into the mug he always used, added the hot water from the teakettle, and set the coffee down before him.

"Thanks," he croaked.

"Welcome," she answered. Then she took the chair opposite him, and the two of them sat there, with only Hank's occasional slurping noises and Elvira's clogged-up breathing breaking the silence. Even the rain was falling silently, it seemed.

Hank had slept little and rested not at all. He knew now, with a cold, hard certainty, what he ought to say to his daughter. But he found himself unable to begin—the words would not form themselves—and the moment passed.

"I got to mail a letter," Elvira said finally. She picked up her envelope.

"Who you got to write?" asked her father.

"The cereal company," explained Elvira. "They got this guarantee on the box, says if you don't like it, you write 'em and they give you your money back. So I'm writin'."

Hank started to laugh, but the laugh turned into a coughing fit.

"You want some water?" Elvira asked, standing up.

"Naw," Hank choked out. "I'm all right. Listen, don't you bother sendin' that letter—it'd be a miracle if you ever heard back from that cereal company. They ain't no guarantees worth piddly squat, and the sooner you figure that out, the better off you'll be."

"Well, I just thought I'd send this, anyway." Elvira

knew better than to disagree with Hank; she looked down at her toes and wondered what had come over her—first the rosebush, now this.

"You sassin' me?" Hank half rose from the table. Elvira shrank back.

"N-no, sir—it don't matter none—if you don't want me to send it, I w-won't."

"Well, all right." Her father settled back down into his chair. "Don't look so scared—it ain't any big deal." He hated the way Elvira cringed every time he raised his voice—as if she thought he might strike her. Why was that, he wondered, when he had never laid a finger on her? He'd sooner have bashed in his own head than hurt a single hair on hers . . .

"I guess I'll go on outside for a while," said Elvira to her toes. "Looks like the rain's let up."

"Yeah, I guess so," mumbled Hank, feeling uncomfortable.

Elvira started for the door.

"Listen . . ." began Hank, groping for the right words.

"Yessir?" Elvira turned around, expecting another lecture.

"Well, I just wanted to . . . you see, there's . . ." The words stuck in Hank's throat. "Aw, shoot, just go on outside. Go on—maybe you could find somebody to play with."

Elvira turned and ran outside. The rain had become

a fine, wet mist that felt good against her skin. Her bare toes wriggled in the warm, squishy mud underfoot. She stopped to check on her rosebush. The blossoms were drooping and dripping from too much of a good thing; yellow petals were scattered like colorful snow on the wet ground.

"It's okay—this rain is gonna make you feel a lot better, you'll see," Elvira whispered to the rosebush. She had heard somewhere once that talking to plants was good for them—was it on Johnny Carson?—but she felt half-ashamed and hoped that no one would notice. "Look here what I got," she continued furtively. "This here's a letter to the cereal company. Hank don't want me to send it, but I'm goin' to, anyway. I don't know why, I just am. Wouldn't it be somethin' if one day the mail came and there was a dollar and forty-nine cents in it for me? Yeah, that'd be somethin', all right. Kind of a late birthday present." As she spoke, Elvira laid caressing fingers on the remaining roses. "See, Hank don't know it's my birthday. I guess he forgot. I ain't gonna tell him, though—he's in a bad mood—it'd just make him feel worse. He'd think he'd have to get me somethin', and he's pretty short on cash right now . . . Well, listen, I got to go—I sure hope you get to feelin' better . . ."

Some kids were messing around in a vacant lot just back of the Happy Trails, but she passed them without a word. The Trumbulls had lived here only a couple of months, and Elvira had never been in any one spot long enough to acquire the knack of making friends. She preferred keeping to herself, anyway. Hank thought that she played with other children—or at least Elvira thought that he thought so—because she always said yes when he asked her if she did. It was simpler that way. Otherwise, Hank would have thought there was something wrong with her, like the time he had yelled at her when that old Mrs. Eloise Willis back in Magnolia had sent home a note on her report card. *Elvira is a little too retiring in class; she seems to be slightly behind in her social development. Please see me*, the note had said.

Hank hadn't seen her; he had said he wouldn't stand for any prissy schoolteacher tellin' him how to raise his kid. But he had said plenty about it to Elvira.

"You got to be more outgoin'," he told her. "You got to just walk right up to those kids and look 'em in the eye and be proud—you're a Trumbull; you can do that. And then they'll like you just fine. Believe me, I know . . ."

But he didn't know; he didn't know at all. He didn't know what it felt like to stand up in front of a whole classroom full of strange faces and have to "tell a little about yourself," the way Elvira had had to do on her first day in Mrs. Willis's fourth grade. She had promptly thrown up on Mrs. Willis's new shoes. Somehow, their relationship had never been altogether ideal after that . . . Elvira hadn't minded a bit when she and Hank had left Magnolia and moved down to Angleton, then up to Nacogdoches, then down again to Silsbee, and then over here to Calder, and no teacher had ever had enough time with her to find out whether or not she even *had* a social development. That was just fine with her.

In ten minutes she had reached the U-Totem on the corner of Broadway and West Doty. She went inside and said hello to Mr. Han, the Oriental gentleman behind the counter. Mr. Han smiled and nodded. He didn't speak much English, but Elvira liked him, because he was always so polite, and because he had never once fussed when she came and read magazines without buying anything. Her favorites were the decorating magazines—the ones with all the pretty houses and gardens. She liked to look at the pictures and imagine herself living inside them. Sometimes she would turn to the food sections and read the recipes and think about surprising Hank one day with potted chicken and artichoke hearts or something fancy like that. Of course, she knew she'd never actually do it, because Hank wasn't overly fond of surprises . . .

But today she didn't stop to look at the magazines. She went straight to the stamp machine, pushed a quarter into it, and pulled the lever on the side. The machine spat out a stamp. She stuck it on her envelope, waved good-bye to Mr. Han, and went on her way.

There was a mailbox a little closer into town. Elvira walked over there now and dropped her envelope inside. The metal door clanged shut. "It'd be a miracle," it seemed to echo hollowly. "No guarantees worth piddly squat . . ."

Well, it had only cost her twenty-five cents. That wasn't all that much . . .

We'll just see, Elvira thought stubbornly. It don't hurt none to see.

2

By the time Elvira got her letter mailed, the sun was already sizzling the puddles and turning the July morning into a giant steambath. Elvira walked along aimlessly for a while, kicking an empty Orange Crush can in front of her. She really didn't have anywhere to go. She knew that Hank wouldn't want her hanging around the trailer, if he was still there; he didn't approve of her watching television all day, although he didn't seem to mind doing it himself. Of course, he might be gone by now—out to look for work, maybe.

Hank never stayed too long at any one job, but he knew enough about one thing and another to get hired on temporarily as a mechanic or handyman or carpenter or something—whatever was available—until the old restlessness possessed him again and pushed him on to the next job, the next town. He hadn't found much work since their arrival in Calder, however; his hip had been troubling him again, and except for an odd job here and there, nothing much had come his way. Money was even more scarce than usual—which meant that the rosebush had been folly, indeed—and Elvira knew it was a wonder that Hank hadn't made her take it back.

Now, if I can just get it to stay alive, she told herself, maybe he'll even get to likin' it. It just takes him a while to get used to things . . . When the cereal company sends me that money, maybe I could use it to buy that rose food I saw over at Kroger . . . Roses got to eat, same as people, I guess . . . I wonder if it'd do any good to smash up all them Wheat Crackles and bury 'em in the dirt around the roots . . . Naw, that'd kill it for sure . . .

The can clattered on. Before long, Elvira found herself on the edge of downtown Calder. There were people on the sidewalk—businessmen in suits that looked much too hot for the weather, a couple of ladies with silver-blue hair and shopping bags, a black kid on a bicycle, a worn-out-looking mother with her mouth set in a grim, straight line, dragging a little girl out of Sears—the girl was screaming bloody murder . . .

Nobody paid any attention to Elvira. Nobody knew it was her birthday. She was glad, in a way; it was as if she had a treasure inside her—a mystery—and nobody knew it but her . . .

The Calder Public Library loomed up ahead of her on the corner like a great gray ghost. It was one of the few buildings in town that had survived from the last century. Most of the other really old ones had either fallen down by themselves, been torn down by modernizers, or been blown down by hurricanes. But the Calder Public Library wasn't the sort of building that could be gotten rid of that easily. It had been a Methodist church to start with, built in the old Victorian Gothic style, and it looked more like a fortress than anything else—or a castle, thought Elvira—the Witch's castle in *The Wizard of Oz*, maybe—just sitting there daring anybody to attack it.

Or even to enter it, for that matter. If you were planning to go there, you'd better mean business. Elvira wasn't planning to go.

But then she happened to think about how they might have books in there that would tell about taking care of roses . . . Somewhere in her mind, she could hear the voice of Mrs. Willadene Graves, the fifth-grade teacher back in Nacogdoches, saying, "If you ever want to find out about anything—anything at all—your local library is the place to look first." But *that* library . . . Suddenly Elvira realized she was afraid, and that made her mad. She was eleven years old now, after all—way too old to be such a scaredy-cat! And this was a public library, wasn't it? And she was the public, wasn't she? Sure she was. So she squared her shoulders, stuck out her bony little chin, marched up to the huge double doors, and pulled hard on one of the handles. Too hard—the door opened so easily and quickly that it banged against the wall outside. Elvira felt her cheeks catch fire. A thin-lipped woman at the desk in the middle of the huge room looked up and stared at her. Elvira thought about turning around and walking away, but she decided that would look even dumber, so she swallowed hard and went on inside.

The woman at the desk went back to rearranging some cards in a long drawer. The name plaque on the front of her desk said: MRS. MARY RUTH SLADER. Elvira noticed that she had unusually long, red fingernails that clicked on the cards . . .

"May I help you?" she asked, without looking up. She didn't really sound much like she *wanted* to help.

"Yes, ma'am," Elvira began, but then her courage failed her, and her mouth froze up. She knew she was going to stutter, so she just didn't say anything at all; sometimes that worked pretty well, and the feeling would pass . . .

"All right, then, *how* may I help you?" asked Mrs. Slader, looking up now and peering at Elvira keenly.

Good Lord, thought Elvira, she looks just like the Wicked Witch of the West . . . Maybe this ain't such a hot idea, after all . . .

She started to back away. "N-never m-mind . . ."

Mrs. Slader looked surprised. "Well now, don't run off—I suppose what you want is the children's library. Miss Ivy will know how to help you. You'll find her right up those stairs there. Go on, now—right up those stairs."

She was so insistent that Elvira was too embarrassed to disobey, even though she didn't think she really wanted the children's library. She turned and practically ran up the spiral staircase that led to what used to be the balcony of the church, fussing at herself all the way up: You're a chicken, you know that—nothin' but a chicken . . .

She figured that she'd just walk around the children's department for a minute and act like she was looking at the kids' books, and then slip back down the stairs and out the door when the Witch wasn't looking. But when she got to the top of the stairs, she stopped dead in her tracks. She forgot all about what she had planned to do. She forgot why she had come into the library in the first place. She couldn't help it. There was an angel sitting at the desk in the middle of the children's department.

Not a genuine, card-carrying angel—angels don't have freckles. It was a lady—IVY ALEXANDER, it said on her name plate; "Miss Ivy"—that was what the Wicked Witch had called her. But she was the closest thing to an angel that Elvira had ever seen. She had reddish-gold hair—the color of an angel's halo, eyes as blue as heaven, and a face sweet and pretty enough to turn a real angel green with envy. She looked up at Elvira and smiled, and her smile was warm and bright and—familiar, somehow—the kind of smile people save for old friends. Elvira could hardly believe that such a smile was meant for her; she looked over her shoulder to see if there was someone standing behind her. There wasn't.

"Hello," said Miss Ivy, and her voice was an angel's voice, too—soft and low as liquid music. "May I help you?" They were the very same words that the Wicked Witch had said, but they sounded altogether different coming out of Miss Ivy's mouth.

Elvira didn't say anything; she couldn't—she felt shyer than she had ever felt in her whole life. She just—stood there.

"You know, you're my first customer today," said the angel-lady.

Elvira just—stood there.

Miss Ivy tried again. "Isn't there anything I can do for you?"

Elvira managed to shake her head.

"Well, then, why don't you just take your time and look around—we've got some wonderful new books on display on that shelf right over there . . ."

Feeling like a fool, Elvira nodded and walked to the shelf that Miss Ivy had indicated. She picked up a book and tried to look as if that was what she had intended to do all along, but she didn't even see what it was; she was too busy listening to her own disgusted voice inside her head: What's the matter with you, anyhow? You think she's gonna bite you or somethin'? You got to be the biggest chicken they ever was—first you're a-scared of that other lady 'cause she ain't too pretty, and now you're a-scared of this one 'cause she is—kinda hard to please, ain't you? Now, go on over there and ask her if they got any books about roses—go on—you come this far—it cain't hurt none to ask . . .

After about five minutes of this, she took a deep breath and approached the desk again. Miss Ivy was pasting a pocket in the back of a book. She looked up and smiled her golden smile.

"Did you find anything you like?"

"N-no, ma'am . . ."

"Well, let's look together, all right? I'm sure we

can find something good." Miss Ivy stood up and started to come around the desk.

"Uh, no, ma'am," said Elvira hastily. "It's just—well, I was wonderin'—if y'all—do—do y'all have any books about roses?"

"Roses?" Miss Ivy lifted her pretty eyebrows questioningly. "Do you mean picture books?"

"N-no, ma'am, I mean, well, I guess it'd be all right if there was some pictures in 'em, but, well, I already got me a rosebush, so I know what they look like . . ." Aw, shoot—why cain't I just say what I mean? she asked herself . . .

But Miss Ivy seemed to understand. "Oh, what you want is a book on gardening—something that will tell you how to grow roses?"

"Yes, ma'am, that's it, that's just what I want," Elvira said, tumbling her words out gratefully.

"Well, then, you're a girl after my own heart." Miss Ivy smiled. "I love gardening, too!"

Elvira felt as if she had gotten the right answer in school or said the secret word and won a prize—quite by accident.

"But, you know, I'm not sure that we have the sort of books you need here in the children's department," continued Miss Ivy. "I'll tell you what we'll do—let's check up here first, and if we don't find anything good, we'll go downstairs . . ."

For the next quarter of an hour, Miss Ivy consulted card catalogues and made notes and checked shelves, moving like a silky summer breeze through the musty old building. She even made it smell nicer—fresher and sweeter, like clover and honeybees . . .

It turned out that they did have to go downstairs, but the Wicked Witch couldn't scare Elvira now; she had Glinda, the Good Witch, protecting her.

"Here we are—I believe these are just what you need," said Miss Ivy, leading Elvira to a shelf full of books with titles like *You and Your Garden, Roses for Everyone, A Beginning Gardener's Guide,* and *Year-Round Roses*. Miss Ivy glanced through them, rejecting the ones that looked too hard or too technical.

"What sort of rosebush do you have?" she asked, as she flipped through the pages of *Gardening in the Glorious Southwest*.

"It's a yeller one," said Elvira. "A—a David—no . . ." What was it that man had called it? "A Davidica rosebush!"

Miss Ivy's eyes sparkled with interest. "Davidica—hmm . . . Well, that's new to me. I'm not sure that any of these books mentions that type specifically, but you ought to be able to find something close to it. Anyway, you really treat most roses pretty much the same way—lots of sunshine and well-drained soil and so forth . . . Oh, just look at these pictures—they almost make me want to run home and start pulling weeds . . ."

Elvira had collected a good-sized stack of books by the time they arrived back at the desk in the children's department.

"Now, I believe you're set," said Miss Ivy approvingly. "All we need is your library card."

Elvira's face fell. "I-I forgot—I don't have one."

"Why, that's all right; don't look so worried," Miss Ivy reassured her. "It's easy to get a library card. Look—I've got this whole stack of applications just begging to be filled out. Now, all you have to do is write down your name and age and address and telephone number and the name of your school, and then get your mother to sign her name on the back . . ."

"Don't have no mother," muttered Elvira, squinching her toes uncomfortably and wondering all over again why she had ever come in this library.

"I'm sorry—that was thoughtless of me," said Miss Ivy, ever so gently. "It doesn't have to be your mother, sweetheart. Your father or your legal guardian—any responsible adult's signature will be fine."

Elvira breathed a sigh of relief. "My daddy's a responsible adult. His name is Mr. Hank Trumbull—can I just sign for him?"

Miss Ivy smiled apologetically. "I'm afraid he'll have to do it himself. But I'll keep these books on reserve for you right here until you get him to sign it—maybe you can come back later this afternoon?"

"I-I don't know for sure if he's home right now, but I'll go check," said Elvira, feeling better. "Can—can you keep them books for me till tomorrow, 'case I cain't find him today?"

Something flickered in the blue eyes, but all Miss Ivy said was, "I surely will. I won't let another soul touch them, I promise."

Elvira took an application and started off. She stopped at the top of the stairs and turned around. "Thanks a whole lot," she said shyly.

"You're welcome," said Miss Ivy, looking as if she really meant it.

All of a sudden, Elvira wanted Miss Ivy to know her secret—she wanted one other person in the world to know—just one . . .

"It's my birthday," she blurted out.

"It is? Well, isn't that nice—happy birthday!" Miss Ivy's smile poured over Elvira like sunshine; it warmed her all the way down to her toes. She was glad she had told.

"Thank you, ma'am."

"Let's see—July twenty-fifth—that means you're a Leo, doesn't it? I've always liked Leos—such strong personalities."

Elvira didn't know what a Leo was, but she was

glad she was one, if Miss Ivy liked them. She flushed with pleasure.

"Well, 'bye."

" 'Bye, birthday girl. You come back soon."

"Yes, ma'am." Elvira turned and ran down the spiral stairs, holding on tightly to the little white card.

3

Elvira ran most of the way home. Her heart was as light as cotton candy. She hardly noticed the heat; the sun was high and hot in the sky now, sending down spiteful rays that baked the sidewalk and scorched her toes, but Elvira didn't care. It was her birthday, and she was a Leo, and everything was fine.

She didn't hear the sound of the television set when she got to the trailer, so she assumed that Hank wasn't home. This was disappointing, even though she had figured he might be gone; she hadn't been able to keep from hoping that she could get that library card and those books today. It didn't really matter all that much; tomorrow would be all right. Still, today would have been nice . . .

She opened the door and went inside. To her surprise, Hank was there after all, sitting on his big chair in the cramped living room area. He was just sitting there, staring into space.

"Hi," she called out cheerfully.

He muttered something in reply; Elvira couldn't quite make it out.

She thought of the library card. "Could you please sign this right here?" She handed him the application and pointed to the proper place.

"I don't have no pen," mumbled Hank.

"Oh, that's all right, I'll get one." Elvira found her old ball-point and held it out to him, too. He signed absently and was about to hand the slip of paper back to Elvira when he seemed to come to and stare at it blankly.

"What's this here I just signed?"

"It's—it's just an application for a liberry card," said Elvira nervously. She wondered why she should feel nervous; surely Hank wouldn't mind her having a library card. But there was something wrong—she could tell.

"Oh. Well, all right," Hank said, handing over the application. "But I don't know that you really need it."

"Yessir, I do," said Elvira anxiously. "I sure do need it. I cain't check out no books without it . . ."

"Yeah, I know. Well . . ." Hank's voice trailed off, and there was a moment's silence.

"So, it's—it's all right, then?" asked Elvira.

"What?" asked Hank. He looked as if he had already forgotten what they were talking about.

"The liberry card," Elvira said patiently. "It's all right for me to have it?"

"I guess so, for the time bein' . . . Look, Elvira, we got to talk."

Something about the way he said this made Elvira's stomach roll over. But then, she was a little hungry . . . "Yessir?" she said.

Hank cleared his throat. "I've just been talkin' on the telephone—to your Aunt Darla . . ."

Aunt Darla. Well, that would explain a lot; talking to Aunt Darla always put Hank in a terrible mood . . .

"You remember your Aunt Darla, don't you?" he continued, a little vaguely.

"Yessir." It was impossible not to remember Aunt Darla, though Elvira would just as soon have forgotten all about her. She was Hank's older sister, a huge, hook-nosed mountain of a woman who was inclined to call Elvira her "poor little motherless Ellie" and cry big slobbery tears all over her. Elvira didn't like her one little bit.

"Well, like I said, I was just talkin' to her, and she says that your Uncle Roy and Roy Jr. and her might be comin' through here in about six weeks—somewhere around the end of August . . ." Hank's voice trailed off again; he seemed to be having a hard time saying what he wanted to say.

"Yessir?" said Elvira, trying to help him out.

Hank cleared his throat uncomfortably. "Well, you know, they got a big old house up there in Sulphur Springs . . . Well, I'm forgettin' myself—you been to that house, ain't you? You remember that Christmas we spent up there . . ."

"Yessir." Elvira remembered that Christmas, all right. She had been eight years old, and she had worn the new dress that Hank had bought for her especially for the holiday. It was red with white trimming—$14.95 at K-Mart—a lot for Hank to be spending—and Elvira had felt real proud and pretty . . . until she had overheard Aunt Darla (who had dressed her substantial self in red, too, so that she looked an awful lot like a giant-sized version of a molded Jell-O salad that Elvira had seen one time at the Piccadilly Cafeteria) talking to Uncle Roy in the kitchen . . .

"Did you see that tacky little dress he's got her in?

It just breaks my heart, that's all . . . He don't have any idea about how to do for a little girl, and I intend to tell him so, too . . ."

Elvira hadn't waited to hear any more, but she had hated Aunt Darla after that. She hated her for saying her dress was tacky and for calling her Ellie and for being so fat. And she hated Uncle Roy and Roy Jr., too—she hated them for their identical boringness; it seemed to her that all they ever did was nod their twin pinheads and agree with everything Aunt Darla said. And she hated the white plastic Christmas tree, and she hated the taco casserole they had had for Christmas dinner—whoever heard of taco casserole for Christmas dinner?—and she had been glad beyond belief when Hank had quarreled with Aunt Darla and had taken Elvira and slammed out of the house long before the day was over . . .

But all she said to Hank now was, "Yessir, I 'member."

"Well, you liked that house, didn't you?"

Elvira hesitated. It was always easier to say what Hank wanted her to say, and Hank wanted her to say that she liked Aunt Darla's house, though she couldn't imagine why he cared if she did or not. Anyway, she decided that it wouldn't be a lie to say that she liked it; it wasn't the house that she didn't like—it was the people in it.

"Yessir, it was all right."

"Well, I guess so. Your Uncle Roy told me he paid seventy thousand dollars for that house. I guess he's made hisself some money, all right . . . Funny thing, I never did think Roy Bledsoe would ever be worth a nickel . . ."

Hank seemed to be talking more to himself than to Elvira. She wondered why in the world they were having this strange conversation.

"You know, Sulphur Springs is a nice town, too," Hank went on. "A real nice little town . . . Don't you think so?" He looked hard at Elvira now, as if it really mattered to him what she thought of Sulphur Springs.

"Yessir," said Elvira politely, although she hadn't noticed anything out of the ordinary about Sulphur Springs; it had looked pretty much like all the other towns they had passed through in their wanderings.

There was another pause. Hank seemed to be right on the edge of saying something else—of coming to some point . . . But instead, all he said was, "Well, I was just—just wonderin' what you thought about it, is all . . ." He got heavily to his feet.

Hank's head was thudding painfully. He hadn't said a third part of what he had intended to say, but he had to get out of the trailer now—it felt like it was closing in on him—he just had to get out for a while . . .

"I got to go see a man about some work," he said in a strained voice. "I'll—I'll see you later on, all right?"

"All right."

Well, he sure was actin' peculiar, thought Elvira, once Hank had gone. It was like—like he had somethin' else on his mind the whole time . . .

Suddenly, a wonderful thought struck her. I bet he's thinkin' about my birthday, she told herself. I bet he's gonna surprise me, like on that old "I Love Lucy" show, when Lucy thought Ricky and Fred and Ethel had all forgotten about her birthday, and then it turned out they were plannin' on surprisin' her all the time . . . I bet that's it, all right—all that talk about Aunt Darla and her house and Sulphur Springs—that was just to throw me off the track . . . Well, I'll hafta act real surprised, even though I already figured it out. He'd be real disappointed if I let on that I knew all along . . .

She decided to wait and go back to the library the next day. She didn't want to be downtown when Hank got home, just in case. She fixed herself some tuna fish. Celery seed and mayonnaise—that was all she put in it—that was the way she and Hank liked it. No onions. Elvira hated onions. Aunt Darla probably puts onions in her tuna fish, Elvira reflected, as she mixed it up. She put the tuna fish between two slices of bread, and then another idea came to her. She'd have herself a picnic. There was a hill just a little way down the road—not a real hill—this was the flattest of flat country—just a little mound of earth that had been piled up by the bulldozers when the highway was built. But it looked pretty much like a real hill now that grass and clover and a few stumpy trees and bushes had grown up on it. Elvira liked to go over there sometimes and sit and just sort of think things over. She could easily see the entrance to the trailer park from there, so she'd be able to see when Hank got back, and she could run home in five minutes. That would make the surprise even better, if she gave him a chance to set it all up. And then she'd come running in, acting like she didn't suspect a thing . . .

She packed her lunch and walked to the hill, humming a little as she went.

There was a big old ant bed right on thc top of that hill. Black ants—not red ones—not the biting kind. Elvira wasn't one bit scared of them; they were sort of pets of hers. She sat down beside the ant bed and ate her sandwich and drank her Thermos-ful of milk, and then she took a stick and poked a few tiny holes in the bed. The ants came pouring out.

"Okay, now, y'all don't get mad—look, I brought you some lunch." She dropped the crumbs of her sandwich down where the ants couldn't miss them, and then she watched as the ants poked and prodded and worried over the crumbs. "Look—you missed one over here . . . That's it—there you go . . . Oh, you're just showin' off—you ain't big enough to carry that all by yourself . . . Well, look at that, you got some muscles, don't you? Naw, you leave him alone, now—he got it first . . ."

She liked the ants. She liked to wonder about them—if they ever thought about anything . . . She had this idea that maybe they had set up little tiny ant temples underground, where they preached about the great goddess Elvira and prayed to her to keep on sending down manna from heaven . . . Elvira had learned about manna from heaven a long time ago, when her mother used to make her go to Sunday school. Elvira wasn't all that religious herself. The only person she had ever known to be really gone on God was Noreen Able, and that wasn't saying much for God; nobody with a lick of sense ever put any stock in anything that came out of Noreen Able's mouth.

Noreen Able had sat in front of Elvira in Miss Reba Foxworth's class in Angleton. Noreen claimed to be a close personal friend of the Holy Ghost. She used to brag that He had inspired her on at least five separate occasions, and that, on the last one, she had spoken in tongues. Elvira had never believed a word of it . . .

She sat on the hill a long time, watching the ants with one eye and keeping the other one on the highway and the entrance to the trailer park, so she wouldn't miss Hank's pickup truck. The sun beat down on her head. The sky was blue as blue could be; not a trace was left of the early morning rain.

She sat there for a long, long time . . . The pickup didn't appear. Finally the sun sank, away off to the left, over toward Houston. The sky turned reddish-pink, then purple, and the first stars glimmered in the gathering darkness.

Star light, star bright,
First star I see tonight,
I wish I may, I wish I might
Have the wish I wish tonight.

She was too old for nursery rhymes, but they were always running through her head. Her mother used to read them to her out of an old book with a checkered cover—over and over and over again . . . *I wish I may, I wish I might . . .*

Well. It had been silly of her to think that Hank was going to surprise her. He had just flat forgotten, that was all.

It didn't matter. Birthdays didn't really matter, except to little kids—cakes and candles and birthday wishes and all that stuff—that was for little kids.

She walked back home after a while. It was past suppertime, so she fixed herself another tuna fish sandwich. She ate half of it, wrapped the other half in tinfoil, and put it in the ice box. She turned on the television. Nothing very good was on. Everything was reruns this time of year. Don Rickles was hosting "The Tonight Show"; Elvira didn't care for him as much as she did for Johnny Carson. *The Sands of Iwo Jima* was on channel thirty-nine; Hank would have liked that, but he wasn't home yet, and Elvira didn't feel much like watching it by herself—she and Hank had already seen it about forty-seven times.

She brushed her teeth. Hank always made a big deal out of her brushing her teeth; he said he couldn't afford dentist bills. She probably should have taken a shower—Hank was big on showers, too—but suddenly she was too tired to do anything else; she was tireder than she had ever been in her whole life. She climbed into bed, and sleep started tumbling everything together in her head . . . 'Bye, birthday girl, you come back soon . . . No guarantees worth piddly squat . . . You, too, can have year-round roses . . . *Star light, star bright* . . . Make a wish, baby—don't you want to make a wish? . . . It don't matter, Mama—my birthday's over, anyhow . . .

4

Elvira woke up the next morning in a foul humor. The air was hot and heavy and generally disagreeable, and it smelled funny, too. The wind must be blowin' from over by that old Goodyear plant again, she thought disgustedly.

Hank was still asleep. Elvira supposed he had been out late again last night. This worried her a little; Hank didn't usually stay out late like that two nights in a row . . .

She walked outside with a drink of water for her rosebush. The last of the yellow blossoms had fallen off, and the leaves were beginning to break out in ugly, brown splotches.

"You don't look too good," she told it irritably, as she poured the water in the dirt around it. "What's the matter with you, anyhow?"

She started to go back inside the trailer, but then she stopped and sighed and turned around half-apologetically. "Look, I'm gonna get some books that'll tell me how to do for you. They got 'em over at the liberry. I'm fixin' to go right now, so you just sit tight till I get back, you hear me? Don't you dare die."

She went inside, got the library card application, and was on her way out the door again when a picture of Miss Ivy floated in front of her mind—she could see her just as clearly as anything, all sweet and pretty and ladylike. And suddenly Elvira was conscious of her own dirty feet and grubby fingernails.

It don't matter, she told herself—nobody cares what you look like—she prob'ly wouldn't even notice.

But all the same, she went back to the bathroom and took a quick shower. She even washed her hair and cut her fingernails.

Well, that's a big improvement, she told her reflection when she was done. Now you got sawed-off fingernails and hair that looks like wet string. But at least you're clean.

And at least today she wasn't afraid of the old gray castle/church/library. It didn't look any less forbidding than it had the day before, but Elvira felt older and wiser now . . . She went inside, looked sideways at the Wicked Witch of the West (Why, she ain't a witch atall, thought Elvira—she's just ugly as homemade sin, poor thing), and climbed the spiral stairs fearlessly.

Miss Ivy was by the window. "Good morning, glory," she called, when she saw Elvira. "Don't you look nice today!"

Elvira flushed. So Miss Ivy had noticed, after all.

"Thanks," she murmured.

"I was sorry you didn't make it back yesterday afternoon, but I hope you were busy having a good time—was it a nice birthday?"

"Yes, ma'am," said Elvira. "It was all right . . ." The words sounded pretty lame and lonesome, and suddenly she found herself embellishing. "My daddy, uh, he—he took me out to eat."

"Oh, how nice!" exclaimed Miss Ivy. "Where did you go?"

"Oh, uh, well—I-I cain't remember, exactly—the—the name of it, I mean—I think it was—well, it was a M-Mexican restaurant . . ."

Elvira wished the earth would open up and swallow her; the way she was blushing and stammering, any fool could see that she was lying through her teeth . . .

But apparently Miss Ivy wasn't just any fool—or, if she was, she surely didn't let on that she had noticed anything. Her blue eyes didn't even blink. "Well, that must have been quite a treat," was all she said, and then she changed the subject. "I've still got your rose books here, safe and sound. Were you able to get your application signed?"

"Yes, ma'am," said Elvira, handing it to her.

"Wonderful," said Miss Ivy, as she looked it over. "Elvira—why, what a pretty name! I don't believe I've ever met an Elvira before."

"Me, neither," said Elvira. "I mean—'cept for me . . ." Well, that was a dumb thing to say, she thought. But Miss Ivy didn't seem to think so . . .

"I'm the only Ivy I know, too," she said. "I was always glad of that." She smiled, and suddenly Elvira felt sure that an unusual name was a fine thing to have.

"All right, Elvira, this will only take a minute . . ." Miss Ivy got out another card and typed all the information from Elvira's application onto that . . . Then she put that card in a little boxy machine that made a peculiar punching noise when she stuck some other cards in it . . . Then she put date-due cards in all the pockets of the rose books . . . Finally, she handed the stack of books to Elvira. "They're all yours," she said. "At least, for two weeks."

"Thank you, ma'am." Elvira hesitated. She was glad to have the books, but she really didn't feel all that much like leaving; she almost wished she had some other excuse to hang around. But she couldn't think of any.

"Well, 'bye," she said, after a minute.

"Good-bye, Elvira," said Miss Ivy. "Hurry back and tell me how your garden grows."

Elvira smiled. That old nursery rhyme—that had been in her mother's checkered book, too . . .

"Yes, ma'am," said Elvira. "I sure will."

For the next few days, Elvira's head swam with Floradoras and Charlotte Armstrongs and Crimson Glories and Red Pinocchios. She read about roses from morning till night; she even skipped Johnny Carson to find out the difference between an everblooming hybrid and a hybrid perpetual, just in case it mattered. She read till her eyes ached, but nowhere in any of those books could she find one word about a Davidica rose. She began to suspect that the slick-haired man who had sold it to her had just made it up. But whatever her rosebush was, it was no wonder that it was dying; the more Elvira read, the more clearly she saw that she had made enough mistakes to kill off any rose grown on the planet earth.

In the first place, she should never have bought a plant with the flowers already on it. That wasn't the way to do it at all. The flowers were supposed to come later. And she should never have planted it during the summer; the books all said that you should plant roses in the spring—or maybe in the fall, in a pinch—but never, never in the heat of the summer . . . And then the soil was all wrong—it should have been "a rich, deep loam," or "a balanced combination of soil, sand, and gravel, mixed with some well-rotted manure"—not just plain old Texas dirt. And she had planted it all wrong, too; she should have made the hole deeper, so that no roots were lying flat . . .

"I'm sorry," she apologized to the rosebush, when she had exhausted all the books and not found much comfort in any of them. "I sure didn't mean to hurt you—I never wanted to do that." She picked up a withered leaf and turned it over in her hand. "Maybe if I start again, you'll do a little better. At least I can dig a deeper hole for your roots—I sure can do that. But I cain't do anything about it being summer, and I just don't know where I'm gonna get you that stuff you need . . . You really ought to have some of that well-rotted manure . . . I don't know, maybe buryin' them Wheat Crackles around you wouldn't have been such a bad idea . . . But don't you worry, you hear me? I'll figure out somethin' . . ."

That afternoon, she walked back over to the library.

The books seemed a lot heavier than thcy had when she had taken them home. They weren't even close to being due, but she didn't want them around her anymore—they made her feel like a murderer every time she looked at them, with their full-color illustrations of gorgeous, healthy roses and their impossible rules about how to grow them.

"Why, Elvira, it's nice to see you again," said Miss Ivy, when the girl plunked the books down on the desk. "Don't tell me you're already finished with all of these!" Her tone was admiring.

"Yes, ma'am, I read 'em all." Even though she was feeling kind of low, Elvira was glad that Miss Ivy was impressed. And she had remembered her name, too—that was something, wasn't it?

"Well, my goodness—you're quite a reader, aren't you? I hope they helped you."

Elvira really didn't feel as if they had helped much, but she didn't want to hurt Miss Ivy's feelings—she had worked so hard to help her find them. So she said, "Yes, ma'am—they—they did fine."

"Oh, good," said Miss Ivy. "I'll bet your roses are going to be just beautiful now."

"Yes, ma'am, I guess so; they'll be real pretty. I mean, they'll be—well, they'll be . . ." She stopped. A picture of her rosebush, all scraggly and pitiful, had just come into her mind, and she couldn't say any more; the lie stuck in her throat.

"Is something wrong, sweetheart?" The blue eyes were so full of kindness that Elvira couldn't bear to look into them. She shook her head and stared down at her bare toes; she had been too depressed to bother with shoes today.

"I'm sure we could find other books," said Miss Ivy gently, "if those were too technical . . ."

Elvira shook her head again. "No, ma'am—it ain't the books—they're all right . . ." She hesitated. "It's just—well, growin' things is harder than I thought—I didn't know there'd be so many rules."

Miss Ivy smiled. "You know, you'd be surprised how many rules I've broken. But my flowers just keep coming up, in spite of me."

Elvira looked up hopefully. "They do?"

"Yes, they do," said Miss Ivy. She looked thoughtful. "I wonder . . ."

"Yes, ma'am?"

"I was just wondering—if maybe you'd like to come by and see them sometime—my flowers, I mean. I might be able to give you a couple of ideas."

Elvira just stood there with her mouth hanging open.

"You'd really be doing me a favor," Miss Ivy went on. "I love to show off my garden, and nobody's paid it a bit of attention lately . . ."

Just then a mother came struggling upstairs with a bald-headed baby on one hip and an armload of books on the other. "I'm so sorry," she said to Miss Ivy, "but these are three weeks overdue . . ."

"I'll be right with you," Miss Ivy said, stopping to scribble something down on a slip of paper. "Here, Elvira—here's my address—Twenty-four-ten South—do you know where that is?"

Elvira nodded dazedly.

"Now, you'll be sure and come, won't you? I'll tell you what—why don't you come this Thursday afternoon—the library is closed that day . . . We'll pretend we're British and have tea, and then we can talk about roses to our hearts' content."

Elvira thought she must be dreaming, but she managed to nod, take the slip of paper from Miss Ivy's hand, and stumble toward the stairs. The bald-headed baby started to cry, and his mother started to talk, but all Elvira heard was Miss Ivy's voice floating out after her as she climbed down the spiral staircase—"See you Thursday, Elvira!" . . . Thursday, Elvira . . . Thursday, Thursday, Thursday . . .

5

Thursday was the day after tomorrow—only two days away—hardly any time—just an eternity, that was all. One minute, Elvira thought the time would never pass; the next, she was terrified that it would. She wanted to go—she had to go—but terrible thoughts kept parading across her brain like old horror movies on the television screen—what if she spilled tea all over herself or put too much food in her mouth or said things so dumb that Miss Ivy would tell her to go on home—she couldn't be bothered with anybody so stupid—what then? Elvira worried until she was almost sick . . .

On Wednesday night she dreamed she was sitting at her desk in Mrs. Eloise Willis's fourth-grade class in Magnolia, when she suddenly discovered that she had forgotten to get dressed. Oh, my Lord, she thought, I'm neckid as a jaybird—no tellin' what Mrs. Willis is gonna say about my social development now . . . She woke up feeling as if she had a whole pack of acrobats turning cartwheels in her belly.

She got up and fixed herself some Cream of Wheat; she thought that the iron in it would settle her stomach and make her feel stronger, but she was wrong—oh, boy, was she ever wrong . . .

Hank knocked on the door while she was in the bathroom throwing up.

"Elvira, are you all right?"

"Yessir, I'm f-fine," she answered, in between gags.

"Well, it don't sound like you're fine. You better go on back to bed, now, you hear me?"

"No, sir—I'm fine, really—I-I just ate too quick, is all . . ."

"Well, maybe so, but it won't hurt you none to stay in bed for a day. I'll move the television over where you can look at it."

Elvira threw open the door and glared at her father. "I ain't s-sick, and I ain't goin' to bed. I c-cain't." She was so upset that she was almost hollering.

Hank was too surprised to be angry. "What do you mean, you cain't?"

Elvira stuck out her chin. "I got somewhere to go today." There was a mixture of pride and defiance in her tone that made Hank cock his head and look at her suspiciously.

"Where you got to go that's so important?"

"To—to a tea party."

"A *tea* party?" Hank looked incredulous for a moment, but then his face relaxed, and a pleased expression came over it. "Well, you musta made yourself a friend, huh?"

"Y-yessir . . ." It was true. Elvira hadn't put it into so many words before, not even to herself, but it was true—Miss Ivy was her friend.

"What's her name?"

"Miss Ivy—Miss Ivy Alexander."

"*Miss?* Well, ain't we gettin' grown-up and fancy all of a sudden?" Hank grinned. It was obvious that he thought Miss Ivy was some little kid. Well, let him think that, if he wants to, Elvira told herself—then maybe he won't be so worried about my social development . . .

"Does this, uh, *Miss* Ivy—does she live in the trailer park?"

"No, sir, she lives in town. I—I met her at the liberry."

"The liberry, huh?" Hank looked impressed. "Well, then, she ought to be right nice—smart, I bet."

"It's all right if I go, then? I-I really ain't sick—I'm already feelin' a whole lot better."

"Well, maybe so. But you ought to lie down for a while, anyhow . . . You don't hafta go over there this early, do you?"

"No, sir, not till this afternoon."

"All right, then. You get back in bed for a little while. There's a real good movie comin' on at ten . . ."

The movie was *The Man Who Shot Liberty Valance*. Hank moved the TV over and then pulled his chair around next to Elvira's bed so he could watch it with her. They didn't talk at all, but it was a comfortable sort of morning, with just the two of them sitting there together watching John Wayne and Jimmy Stewart and Lee Marvin and those other old guys shooting each other all to pieces. It took Elvira's mind off the tea party, and that was a relief. When the movie ended, Hank told her to stay in bed just a little longer; he had to go somewhere, but he'd be right back . . .

Sure enough, he was back pretty soon; he had gone over to Kroger and bought some tomato soup. He fixed it up and carried it to Elvira on a tray with some crackers. Her stomach was feeling better now; she ate the soup gratefully.

"Thank you, sir—that was real good," she said, when she had finished.

Hank looked embarrassed. "You're welcome," he mumbled. He put an awkward hand on Elvira's forehead. "Well, it don't feel like you got a fever. I guess it's all right if you go on over to your friend's house. What time you s'posed to go?"

"All she said was afternoon—I don't know what time exactly," said Elvira, wrinkling up her forehead into worried lines. She hadn't thought to get the time clear. "She just said we'd have tea—like we was British people—b-but I don't know what time they have tea . . ."

"Oh. Well, that'd be about four o'clock," said Hank, to his daughter's astonishment.

"How do you know that?" Elvira's eyes were wide.

Hank chuckled. "Surprised you, huh? I guess I know a trick or two I ain't showed you yet . . . Well, matter of fact, when I was growin' up back in Sulphur Springs, the folks next door were from over in England. The Sharps—I'll never forget 'em—Ol' Man Sharp owned the hardware store . . . They had a boy—Whitney, his name was; he was my best friend . . . Lordy—Whitney Sharp—haven't thought about him in years . . . We had us some good times, ol' Whitney and me—even courted the same girl when we got to high school . . ." Hank's voice had gotten sort of low and dreamy while he talked—it was an awful lot of talk for him—and now it trailed off altogether . . .

"The girl y'all courted—was that my mama?" asked Elvira timidly.

Hank seemed to come back to himself. He cleared his throat uncomfortably. "Uh, yeah—it was your mother . . . Look, I believe I'll stop on by the Davis Lumber Company—I heard they might be hiring over there . . . You feelin' all right now, huh?"

"Yessir."

"Well. All right, then. You mind your manners at that tea party, you hear me? I guess I'll see you later on . . ."

Elvira lay in her bed for a while longer. Now that she knew tea was supposed to be at four o'clock, she had plenty of time. She wasn't feeling so nervous now; it seemed that something of Hank's reverie had spilled over. She thought of him and Whitney Sharp dating the same girl back in high school . . . her mother . . . Elvira wondered why Hank had never talked about that before. Matter of fact, he never talked about her mother at all . . . But then, lately, he had been acting kind of strangely, it occurred to Elvira. Quieter, and just—different, somehow. Sometimes she would look up and he'd be staring at her, with a funny expression in his eyes . . . Well, there was no figuring Hank. He was just—Hank, that was all.

6

Miss Ivy lived on a quiet street in one of Calder's older neighborhoods. Elvira knew right where it was; she had passed South Street dozens of times on her way into town. The houses along it were mostly big and old-fashioned, with wide front porches and two, sometimes even three, stories. Huge shade trees arched their branches far overhead; they looked as if they had been standing there for a long, long time, like giants locked in a never-ending game of London Bridge . . .

Two little kids raced by, one on a bicycle, the other on a kind of plastic tricycle with a great big yellow front wheel. The smaller kid was wearing a black space helmet and carrying a green plastic baseball bat. There was a bright blue bath towel pinned around his neck—it streamed out in back of him while he pedaled furiously after the boy on the bike.

Elvira walked slowly and breathed slowly and willed her heart to slow down, too, but it wasn't much use. Her nervousness had come back full force the minute her Keds had pointed themselves down South Street. She was holding the slip of paper with the address on it—she knew it by heart, but the paper was proof that she hadn't just dreamed the whole thing up . . .

And then she was there, and her heart didn't just slow down—it seemed to stop beating altogether.

Twenty-four-ten was a cozy-looking white house with green shutters on the windows. A wooden swing, touched by the breeze from an old-timey ceiling fan, creaked invitingly over on one side of the porch. A fat yellow cat sunned itself comfortably on the roof. It was a nice house—just the sort of house that Miss Ivy ought to live in. But it wasn't the house so much that made Elvira's heart skip a beat—what really got her were the roses. There were roses all over the place—wonderful roses—red ones and pink ones and, oh, yes, yellow ones—glorious roses . . . There were other flowers, too—beds full of them—but Elvira hardly saw them; she was drowning in roses . . . She just stood there, staring, practically drooling . . .

But just then the kid on the bike and the other one in the space helmet came pedaling furiously back up the sidewalk. The big one stopped right in front of her. He was a curly haired, freckle-faced boy of about eight, maybe nine.

"Are you Elvira?" he asked, out of the blue.

"Uh-huh," she murmured blankly. How in the world did this kid know her name?

"Well, I'm Curtis," the boy went on. "Curtis Alexander. The third," he added, as an afterthought. "This is my brother, John David Alexander.

" 'Lo," said a voice from inside the space helmet.

"Take off the helmet, John David," said Curtis, nudging his brother.

"Why?"

" 'Cause it's polite."

"Oh." The little boy removed his helmet and grinned bashfully at Elvira. He had straight, dark hair that hung low on his forehead and almost hid his blue eyes.

"Go tell Mama the company's here," said his brother.

The little kid turned around and ran into the house—Miss Ivy's house. Elvira stared after him stupidly. Then she turned back to his brother; he had said their last name was Alexander . . .

"Are y'all kin to Miss Ivy?" she asked him.

Curtis looked surprised. "Well, sure—she's our mother. She told us to look out for you."

Their mother . . . somehow, Elvira had never thought of Miss Ivy as anybody's mother . . . Angels didn't have kids, did they?

"I-I didn't know she was married—I thought she was a miss . . ."

Curtis looked embarrassed. "She's not married—not anymore," he muttered. "Well, come on in the house. She's waitin' for you."

Elvira was mortified. She wished she hadn't said anything. She followed Curtis inside, resolving to keep her mouth closed in the future.

The inside of Miss Ivy's house was everything that it should have been. The front room was big and sunny—a real living room, meant for living in. There were plants and flowers everywhere and comfortable-looking furniture and bookcases filled with books and a piano in the corner and a beautiful old fireplace . . . Miss Ivy's house, thought Elvira, breathing it all in—why, it's like one of them pictures in *Better Homes and Gardens* . . . Maybe not so fancy, but just as nice—nicer, even—homier . . .

And then Miss Ivy herself came down the stairs,

looking bright and happy as an angel ought to look. She was wearing a yellow blouse and white slacks and a pair of sandals that showed off her graceful little feet. Her halo hair was pulled back in a ponytail and tied with a blue ribbon that matched her eyes . . . Lordy, thought Elvira, if I could look like that for just one single day of my life, I'd die happy . . . You couldn't hardly ask for more than that . . .

"I'm so glad you could come, Elvira," Miss Ivy was saying. "Did you meet Curtis and John David?"

"Yes, ma'am."

"Well, good. You know, I couldn't remember if I had told you about my boys before . . ."

"No, ma'am—I was real surprised—you don't look that old . . ." Elvira stopped and cringed; that hadn't come out right at all.

But Miss Ivy only laughed a friendly kind of laugh and said, "Well, that's a nice compliment—thank you."

Elvira took a deep breath and tried to do better. "I saw your flowers outside—they're real beautiful."

"Oh, do you like them? I'm so glad—the boys have helped me with them a lot, haven't you, boys?"

"I hate weeds," said Curtis, rolling his eyes.

"Me, too," chimed in John David.

"I'm a slave driver—that's what I am," chuckled Miss Ivy. "You'd better watch out, Elvira—I'll have you pulling weeds, too."

"I wouldn't mind."

"I don't believe you would, would you? You know, sometimes I get kind of a kick out of it, too. It's good therapy, when I start feeling crazy. But even I don't need *that* much therapy . . . Well, we shouldn't be standing here—it's so hot—you must be thirsty. I thought we'd have our tea out on the side porch; there's a fan out there to keep us from melting, and that way we can enjoy the flowers while we visit."

"Can I have punch 'stead of tea, Mama—I hate tea."

"*May* I have, John David . . . Curtis, will you please bring out the sugar bowl—I believe I left it in the kitchen . . . Do you like tea, Elvira? It's iced tea—I thought that would be better in this hot weather . . ."

It was an altogether elegant tea party. Miss Ivy was the perfect hostess, handing out dainty plates of cucumber sandwiches and fresh fruit and little strawberry tarts . . . Elvira began to wonder what she had been so worried about. It was all so easy, after all—as easy and natural as breathing . . . just sitting there, sipping iced tea as if she did it every day of her life, listening to Miss Ivy talk comfortably about flowers and gardening . . . Until Elvira opened her mouth the wrong way again . . .

"What kind of a rosebush did you tell me yours is?" asked Miss Ivy.

"The man called it a Davidica," answered Elvira, "but I don't know—I never did find one by that name in any of them liberry books."

"Lib*rrrr*ary," began John David. "You're supposed to say lib*rr* . . ."

"Uh, come on in the house with me for a minute, John David," said Curtis, standing up and taking his brother by the arm. "There's, uh, there's somethin' I need to show you."

"What?" asked John David.

"Just somethin'—come on, now—uh, may we be excused?" He looked at his mother.

"Yes, you may," said Miss Ivy, putting a hand on her older son's shoulder. "Thank you, Curtis." She turned back to Elvira. "I just got a new catalogue the other day—why don't we take a look at it? Maybe we'll find your rosebush in there . . ."

"Don't you know *anything*?" came Curtis's voice, quite distinctly, from inside the house . . . and then John David's indignant reply, "What? What'd I do?"

Elvira was as red as one of Miss Ivy's roses, but Miss Ivy acted as if nothing had happened and went on talking so cheerfully that after a while Elvira forgot all about feeling dumb . . .

The catalogue that Miss Ivy brought out was a fat one, filled with pictures and names of hundreds of different flowers and plants. She and Elvira went through the rose section and tried to find the Davidica. It wasn't there.

"But that doesn't mean there's no such thing," explained Miss Ivy. "There are new varieties being developed all the time. I'll tell you what—let's go on out in the garden and look around; you might see a rose that reminds you of yours."

The garden tour was the best part of the visit; Elvira could have sworn she had died and gone to heaven.

"Those are morning glories," said Miss Ivy. "They're all closed up now, but you just come back in the morning sometime and see how pretty they are . . . And that's trumpet vine, and those are impatiens and begonias . . . The tall yellow flowers are daylilies . . . Oh, I wish you could have seen the pinks—they're done now . . . But look over there, hiding behind that hibiscus—can you see the periwinkles? I'm just crazy about periwinkles . . ."

"They're all mighty pretty," said Elvira respectfully. "But I like the roses the best."

Miss Ivy smiled. "You know, I do, too. I feel almost guilty having favorites—sometimes I think it's a little like a parent having favorites—but I can't help it. There's just nothing sweeter than a rose. They're stubborn, too. They may look delicate, but I've seen roses survive when I didn't think there was any way on earth they could."

"Even—even when their leaves turn brown and start fallin' off?" Elvira was ashamed to admit it, but she had to find out.

"Even then," said Miss Ivy, giving her a keen look. "Don't you give up on that rosebush of yours—it's tougher than you think. It doesn't have those thorns for nothing, you know."

"But them books I read—they talked about roses needin' rich, deep loam and well-rotted manure and stuff like that, and—and I believe I planted it wrong, too—"

Miss Ivy looked thoughtful. "Well, it is important to begin well . . . But I'll bet you could rework your bed with some good dirt and a little fertilizer . . . Maybe even dig up your rosebush and then replant it very carefully— It might lose all its leaves, but they'd come back after a while, better than ever . . ."

Elvira sighed and shook her head. "No, ma'am. Dirt and fertilizer—they're—well, they're way too high, that's all there is to it." She tried to sound matter-of-fact; she didn't want Miss Ivy to think she was poor-mouthing.

All of a sudden Miss Ivy's smile flashed out again, radiant as the sun. "Well, that's no problem at all—just come take a look over here."

She led Elvira to a small toolshed that was tacked onto the back of the house. She opened the door. A pungent odor floated out. "What do you think of that?" she asked, her eyes twinkling.

Elvira looked inside. The shed was dim; it took a moment for her eyes to adjust from the bright light outside. But when they did, she gasped—it was a gardener's treasure chest—filled with spades and hoes and shovels and rakes and shears and, best of all, several enormous bags of fertilizer. It smelled horrible, but Elvira already had a gardener's nose—

"Oh, boy, that's the good kind, ain't it?" she breathed reverently.

"Pure gold," laughed Miss Ivy. "I got way too much last spring—I thought I was going to have time to start a new bed, but I never got around to it. I'm a great starter, but not always such a great finisher . . . There's a pile of dirt left, too, over in that corner by the back fence—way more than I'll ever need. Just a little of that should be plenty for your rosebush."

"Oh, no, ma'am—I couldn't take your stuff!"

"Why not? It's just sitting there, not doing anybody one bit of good; I'd much rather have it put to some use."

Elvira took a deep breath. She wanted that stuff, all right; she wanted it so much she could hardly stand it. But, still, she stuck out her chin stubbornly. "I sure do thank you, ma'am, but I cain't take it. My daddy says not to ever take nothin' for free—he says the Trumbulls don't like to be beholden to nobody."

"I see," said Miss Ivy. "Well, I'm sure that's a good rule. But it seems like such a shame . . ." She was quiet for a minute; she was apparently turning something over in her mind. And then her eyes lit up . . . "Oh, Elvira—I know what we can do—it's perfect! How would you like a job?"

"Ma'am?"

"You know how you were saying earlier that you wouldn't mind pulling weeds?"

"Yes, ma'am . . ."

"Well, my boys hate it—they really do—they just don't see the point at all. And I'm at the library so much that it's really hard to find the time to do it myself. Well, don't you see? We could have a trade-off—you could pull weeds for me, when you have the time, and I could let you have whatever you might need for your garden. How would that be?"

It was too good to be true. Elvira was speechless; she could only nod happily.

"Now, are you sure you wouldn't mind the work?" asked Miss Ivy. "It would be such a help to me, I just can't tell you—but weeding can be a real pain . . ."

Elvira managed to find her tonguc. "I-I'd like it—I really would."

Miss Ivy beamed at her. "Great—it's a deal, then. Shall we shake on it?"

It was the kind of day when one good thing was just naturally bound to be followed by another. When Elvira got back to the trailer, Hank was waiting there for her with a bucket of chicken. It had been a long time since they had had fried chicken for supper; Hank usually swore that the Colonel was way overpriced.

"But they was havin' a special over there today," he explained, almost apologetically. "Anyway, I figured maybe we could afford a little treat tonight." He grinned. "You 'member I told you I was goin' over to the lumberyard 'safternoon. Well, they told me to come back tomorrow. I don't know for absolute sure, but it looks like they're gonna put me on full-time."

"That's real good," said Elvira happily. If Hank got steady work, then they'd be staying on in Calder for a long time, and things wouldn't be so tight, and maybe Hank wouldn't keep getting into those strange, starey moods he'd been having lately . . .

For sure, he wasn't in a strange mood tonight. Elvira couldn't remember the last time he had seemed so cheerful. While they ate their chicken, he even joked around a little.

"I met this fella over't the lumberyard today—you know what his name was?"

"No, sir."

"Noah Goode."

Elvira giggled. "Naw . . ."

"No kiddin'—that's his name. Mr. Noah Goode . . . He's a mean son-of-a-gun, too—ain't nobody gonna kid him about his name." Hank chuckled. "I guess when you got a name like that, you got to be either real mean or real nice, like old Ima Hogg . . ."

Elvira choked. "I-Ima Hogg?"

"It's the truth, so help me—there was this rich old lady used to live in Houston—her name was Ima Hogg. They say she had a sister named Yura, too—get it? Ima Hogg and Yura Hogg."

"Aw, you're kiddin' me."

Hank laughed. "Well, I think they's lyin' about Yura, but there really was an Ima; I passed her place over in Houston one time. They say she was a real nice old lady—always givin' money away to charity and such as that . . . People was just crazy about her, called her 'Miss Ima' and all . . ."

They munched contentedly on the chicken for a few more minutes, and then Hank got a teasing look in his eye. "Speakin' of misses, how was your friend today? The one that had that tea party?"

"Oh, she was, uh—she was just fine . . ." Elvira thought momentarily of straightening Hank out about Miss Ivy's age, but she decided against it; he was in such a good mood—no sense in breaking the spell . . . "I'm, uh, I'm s'posed to go over there again tomorrow."

"Well, ain't that nice? I guess there won't be nobody here tomorrow, then—I'll be at work, acourse." Hank said it matter-of-factly, as if it were nothing at all, but Elvira could tell how good he was feeling.

Later on they sat up and watched television together. There was an old horror movie on—*The Blob*—all about how this slimy stuff started taking over the world. It was pretty funny. Or maybe it was just that Hank and Elvira felt like laughing . . .

"Well, I guess we really ought to be gettin' to bed," said Hank, when it was over. "Got to get an early start in the mornin'."

"Yessir, me, too," said Elvira.

"Well, you have a good time with your friend, now. Y'all behave yourselfs. I'll see you when I get home from work."

"Yessir."

"Good night, Elvira."

" 'Night, Daddy."

It had been a long time since she had called him Daddy; she didn't usually call him anything at all. But it felt right tonight. Everything felt right tonight.

7

August was born even hotter than July, but Elvira didn't care. She had never been happier. She went over to Miss Ivy's on Friday and Saturday and again on Monday to pull weeds. It was hard, sticky work, all right, but every weed uprooted was like money in the bank for her rosebush. And it was more than that, too. The way she felt went beyond her hope for the rosebush; she felt good and peaceful and so completely . . . at home—that was the only way she could describe it. She liked squatting on her hands and knees in the good, rich dirt of Miss Ivy's garden, with the scent of Miss Ivy's flowers all around her and the contented buzzing of Miss Ivy's bees in her ears. She liked working until she was hot and sweaty and then turning on the sprinkler and lying on the grass beneath it, so that she and the plants could cool off together. And she liked it best of all when Miss Ivy came home, and they'd sit and talk as the late afternoon shadows fell across the garden . . .

Sometimes, while Miss Ivy was off at the library, her boys would come out and help with the weeding. They were home most of the time; a nice old lady named Mrs. McFaddin minded them while their mother was at work. Mostly Mrs. Mac would sit in the house and watch television, while the boys played outside. For some reason, it didn't take Elvira any time at all to get used to having Curtis and John David around. She didn't feel as shy with them as she did with other kids. Maybe it was because they were younger than she was, but more likely it was just because they belonged to Miss Ivy. And they were pretty good company, too, although they really weren't all that much help; John David would get bored and start fooling around in about five minutes' time, and Curtis obviously didn't know what in the world he was doing . . .

"Don't pull those up, Curtis—those are flowers—don't you see them little red buds on the tips?"

"Are those red?"

"Sure they are—cain't you see?"

"Curtis is color-blind," explained John David, who was lying on his stomach in the grass, trying to catch doodlebugs.

"No kiddin'—you cain't see colors?" asked Elvira, sitting up straight and looking at Curtis with interest.

"Nope. At least, not the same way you see 'em."

"You mean it's like—like lookin' at black-and-white television?"

"Aw, it's not that bad. It's mostly just reds and greens and browns that sort of blend in together. It's really called shade blindness. I got it from my daddy." Curtis sounded almost proud of his affliction.

"I don't think you can get that from your daddy," said Elvira. "There was this kid in my school last year—he did a report on it in science. He said a boy gets it from his mother, only she don't really have it—she just passes it down from her daddy, or somethin' like that . . ."

"Well, he was wrong, that's all," said Curtis positively. "I got it from my daddy."

"Well, all right, you don't have to get mad about it." Elvira shrugged her shoulders and turned back to her work.

"Who said I was mad? I'm not mad," said Curtis,

pulling up a baby salvia that shouldn't have been pulled up.

"Our daddy's gonna take us to Astroworld week after next," said John David. "We're gonna spend a whole week with him in Houston."

"Oh," said Elvira. So Miss Ivy's husband wasn't dead—Elvira had figured him to be dead . . .

"I wish we still lived in Houston," Curtis said, almost to himself.

"Y'all used to live in Houston?" asked Elvira. This was news, too.

"Uh-huh. Till—till a couple years ago."

"I like Calder better," said John David, as he nabbed a slow-witted doodlebug and watched it curl up in a ball in the palm of his hand. "There's not so much traffic, and it's a better place for kids."

"Aw, you're just sayin' that because it's what Mama says," said Curtis disgustedly. "You don't even remember when we lived in Houston—you were just a baby when—well, when we moved here."

"I wasn't either a baby—I was four years old," said John David indignantly. "And I remember just as good as you do . . . Hey, looka here at this roly-poly, Elvira—I got him trained to crawl up my arm."

"Hmmm?" said Elvira, absently jerking up a dandelion root as big as a good-sized carrot. She wasn't really listening anymore; she was trying to imagine what kind of a man would divorce Miss Ivy. He couldn't be in his right mind, that was for sure. Unless maybe she had divorced him . . . but she wouldn't have done that unless he had really deserved it; Miss Ivy wasn't the type that would just walk out on somebody without a plenty good reason. So he had to be either crazy or no-account—that was all there was to it . . .

By Monday afternoon, Elvira had pulled just about every weed she could find in the largest of Miss Ivy's flower beds, and she had begun to make headway on another, when Miss Ivy walked into the garden late that day and sat down beside her.

"I can't believe how much you've gotten done, Elvira—I've never seen anybody work so hard!" she exclaimed, looking around in amazement. "It must be that Leo blood in you—you're fierce when you put your mind to something, aren't you?"

"Oh, I don't know," said Elvira, blushing mightily.

"Yes, you are—a lioness, that's what you are," insisted Miss Ivy. "And the garden shows it—it's never looked more beautiful."

"Thank you, ma'am."

"But you're working *too* hard, sweetheart. You've already done more than enough to earn whatever you want for your garden. I think it's time we evened things up, don't you?"

"But—there are still a lot more weeds in them other beds . . ."

"Bless your heart—I never meant that you had to pull every one of them!" Miss Ivy cried. "You have to leave some for my therapy, you know. And I don't believe we should keep that rosebush of yours waiting any longer, do you?"

That did the trick. "Well, no, ma'am—I guess I do need to tend to it—if you really think I've done my part . . ."

Miss Ivy laughed and put an arm around Elvira's shoulders. "Yes, ma'am, I do—in fact, I would say that I'm in *your* debt now, and we Alexanders don't like to be beholden any more than you Trumbulls do. Now, let's see—Thursday's my day off, so you come over here early Thursday, and we'll load up the car with everything we need . . ."

Miss Ivy's old green Chevy was out in front of the house when Elvira arrived on Thursday morning. A bag of fertilizer and a couple of big boxes of good dirt were already loaded up in back. Elvira found Miss Ivy in the backyard on her knees in one of the flower beds. She was digging. There was another big box half filled with plants on the ground beside her.

"Hi, Miss Ivy—what are you doin'?" Elvira asked curiously.

"Oh, I'm just thinning out some of these fall flowers—they really need it—I don't know why I never got around to it before. I thought maybe the extras could keep your rosebush company. You wouldn't mind taking them off my hands, would you?" Miss Ivy made it sound as if Elvira would be doing her a big favor.

"No, ma'am, I—I wouldn't mind," she stammered.

Curtis and John David came along on the trip over to the trailer park. Elvira was a little nervous about showing the Alexanders the place she lived; she wasn't sure what they'd think about it, coming from a house as nice as theirs . . .

"Wowee—look at that!" cried John David, as the Chevy pulled into the Happy Trails. He was pointing to one of the biggest trailers. "That's fine—I wish we lived in one of those!"

"Boy, that'd be great," agreed Curtis. "Why don't we trade our house in for a trailer, Mama? Then we could live anywhere we wanted to—the Grand Canyon or Disneyland or—or Houston—anywhere at all . . ."

His mother smiled. "I'm pretty well committed to our house for the time being, Curtis. But it would be nice to be that free, wouldn't it?"

"That's ours right over there," said Elvira, pointing to her home. She felt fine about it now—even proud. Miss Ivy and her boys seemed to think that living in a trailer was a real privilege. "And there's my rose-bush," she added, as the car came to a stop.

"Well," said Miss Ivy softly. For a moment she

seemed unable to say anything else; she fumbled around in her purse for a Kleenex and then blew her nose hard. "Excuse me," she apologized. "Allergies . . ." She smiled brightly again. "Well, now, I would say that it looks like we've come in the nick of time. Let's get to work, shall we?"

"Yes, ma'am," said Elvira.

The first thing they did was dig up the rosebush, ever so carefully; Miss Ivy treated it with as much respect as she would the rarest orchid.

"You really think it's gonna be all right?" Elvira asked anxiously, as Miss Ivy examined the barren branches.

"Well, I'd say it still has a good chance," Miss Ivy said. "It's certainly not dead yet—not by a long shot. Look, the branches aren't brittle—they can still bend without breaking. That's a good sign . . . I'd say your rosebush has a very good chance, Elvira."

"It looks deader'n a doornail to me," said John David, shaking his head. "Ouch—what're you kickin' me for, Curtis?"

"Don't kick your brother, Curtis. John David, this rosebush is not dead," said Miss Ivy firmly. "It's just resting, the way plants do in the wintertime."

"Sure hot for wintertime," muttered John David . . .

They worked all that morning—all four of them—even John David, so Elvira had to forgive him for saying the rosebush was dead. They turned over the rock-hard dirt and mixed it with the good stuff and put fertilizer on top of that and then went over everything with spades. Elvira dug a new, deeper hole for the rosebush; together, she and Miss Ivy eased it in tenderly, taking care that the roots were pointing down and out, just as the books had said. When that was done, they put in the other plants from Miss Ivy's garden . . .

"Chrysanthemums and marigolds and Gloriosa daisies," said Miss Ivy, taking off her garden gloves and surveying their handiwork with a satisfied air. "They ought to bloom right on through fall."

"It's all just perfect," breathed Elvira, her eyes shining. "I cain't believe it's mine . . ."

"It's yours, all right. You earned it, fair and square," said Miss Ivy. "Now, give it plenty of water today, and then just enough every day after that to keep the soil moist—not soggy . . ."

"Yes, ma'am."

"And watch out for weeds, just the way you did for me . . ."

"Yes, ma'am."

"And if you see any bugs that look like they're hurting anything, let me know; we can dust the leaves with something, if we really need to . . ."

"Yes, ma'am."

"And I guess that's all your garden needs—except

love—but I don't need to tell you that, do I?" said Miss Ivy, tucking a loose strand of hair behind Elvira's ear.

"No, ma'am," said Elvira. She would love it, all right. It felt as if her heart would burst, there was so much love inside it.

8

For a good while after Miss Ivy and the boys had gone home, Elvira just sat there on the ground in front of her garden, loving it . . .

It was well past noon when it occurred to her that she was hungry. She went inside and was about to fix herself a can of macaroni and cheese, when the trailer door slammed behind her, making her jump so that she dropped the can and the pan and the spoon in a confused clatter. Hank came into the kitchen. His lips were set in a tight, straight line.

"Got off work early today, huh?" asked Elvira. She meant it to sound cheerful, but the words fell flat. Something was wrong.

"Ain't no more work," muttered Hank. "They gave the job to somebody with friends in high places . . . Never mind about that—where'd you get the money for all that stuff outside?"

"It didn't cost nothin'—I got it from Miss Ivy . . ."

Hank looked perplexed. "You mean that little girl you've been playing with—you got all that dirt and them plants from her?"

"N-no, sir—I guess I never told you—I meant to—Miss Ivy ain't no little girl—she's a lady."

This news didn't make Hank any happier. "What are you sayin' to me, Elvira? Are you sayin' that some strange woman's been givin' you stuff?"

Elvira wasn't about to stand for anyone calling Miss Ivy names—not even Hank—especially not Hank. She drew herself up as tall and straight as she could and made herself look him squarely in the eye. "Miss Ivy ain't strange—she ain't one bit strange. She's a real nice l-lady."

"I don't care if she is nice. We don't take handouts from nobody, not in this family. And I don't appreciate it one bit that you've been deceivin' me, neither—makin' me think you had made yourself a friend, when all the time . . ."

"Miss Ivy is my friend!" Elvira cried. "She's the b-best friend I ever had—and she didn't g-give me no handouts, neither—I worked hard for that stuff—we had a d-deal . . ."

"Don't you raise your voice to me, young lady!" Hank's eyes flashed fire. "You just try and show a little respect, do you hear me? I don't know what's come over you lately . . ." He broke off suddenly and began to pace around the little room, running his fingers distractedly through his hair so that it stood up like question marks on the top of his head. Then, as suddenly as he had started, he stopped pacing and turned to face Elvira; he looked as if he had made up his mind about something. "Look, I guess it's gettin' pretty plain that there's got to be some changes made around here . . . I thought for a while that maybe things would work out, but I was just foolin' myself. I can see that now . . ."

A chilly feeling oozed all over Elvira as he said this—a kind of cold, clammy feeling that made her think of that old movie they had watched on television the other night—*The Blob,* that was it—only it wasn't so funny now. "Changes?" she asked, in a smaller voice.

"That's right, changes. I've been thinkin' it over

some lately—matter of fact, I thought about it a lot, and . . ." Hank stopped, cleared his throat, and then started again. "Well, I was talkin' to my sister on the telephone a couple weeks ago—you remember, I told you I talked to her before . . . Anyway, we agreed—her and me—we decided that maybe it would be better for everybody if you went to live with her and her family in Sulphur Springs." Hank's voice had gotten lower and lower during this speech, so that it finally was hardly more than a whisper, but he might just as well have shouted; the words rained around Elvira's ears like blows. She stared uncomprehendingly at her father.

"D'you hear me?"

"Y-yessir," she managed, with an effort.

"Well, say somethin', then."

"You mean—you mean Aunt Darla?"

"Acourse I do. She's the only sister I got, ain't she? You remember I told you that your Uncle Roy and Roy Jr. and her's gonna be comin' through here on the way back from their vacation . . . Well, we already got it all settled and planned out . . . You'll go on back with them to Sulphur Springs in time for the start of school. You ought to like it just fine over there—you said before how much you liked that house . . ."

That other conversation came back into Elvira's mind . . . It had been on her birthday, hadn't it? Right about the time that Hank had started acting so strangely . . . Or had it been after she got the rosebush—was that when it was? She struggled to make some sense of it all—there had to be some reason . . .

"I-I c-could t-t-t . . ."

"Quit stutterin', Elvira. You got somethin' to say, then say it." Hank didn't usually criticize Elvira's stuttering, but it seemed neither of them could do anything right today . . .

"I could t-take back the rosebush . . ."

"Forget that blasted rosebush!" exploded Hank. "It ain't that . . ."

"Then why?"

"It's just that, well, a girl ought to have a woman around her to teach her about—well, about female kinda things . . ."

Elvira looked up hopefully. "I know about that stuff already, and anyway, I got Miss Ivy now . . ."

"Don't you interrupt me—I don't want to hear no more about Miss Ivy. She's no kin—she's got nothin' to do with this. The Trumbulls don't need nothin' from no outsiders. You got your Aunt Darla—she's family, and she's anxious to have you; she's married to a rich man, and there's just some things she can do for you that I could never . . ."

"I don't care about any of that!" cried Elvira. "I'd ruther stay with you—you're my daddy . . ."

Hank gritted his teeth to ward off the pain; it made

him look fiercer than ever. "You hush, now—didn't I tell you not to interrupt me? You got to pay attention. The truth is . . ." Hank cast about desperately for words that would say all the right things, but none would come, and then he heard himself saying, "The truth is I want you to go, do you hear me? I want you to go . . . So there ain't no use talkin' any more about it."

For a moment, neither of them said anything. Silence hung in the air between them like thick, black smoke . . . Somewhere in the distance, a child laughed. Elvira wondered dully what he had to laugh about.

"You really want me to go?" Her voice was flat.

"That's what I said," muttered Hank shamefacedly. He was glad, for once, that Elvira wasn't looking him in the eye. "You'll do just fine over there, once you get used to it. And your Aunt Darla—she's crazy to have you—she ain't never had a little girl; she'll prob'ly spoil you rotten."

Elvira nodded. Something was happening to her throat. It felt as if somebody had tied a scarf around it too tightly, so that she couldn't speak or swallow—she could hardly breathe . . .

After another pause, Hank spoke again. "Look, I, uh—I got to go out for a while. Don't wait up—I-I might be late . . ." He wanted to get away—he had to get away and hide someplace where the pain couldn't follow him.

Elvira nodded again. She stayed very still, because she felt as if her head had a trillion tiny explosions going on inside it, and any sudden movement might send pieces of her brain flying around the trailer.

Hank coughed and started toward the door. Then he stopped and stood there, struggling with himself. "It's the best thing, you hear me? So don't go actin' like no crybaby."

The trailer door slammed, and he was gone.

No guarantees worth piddly squat. The words swam through Elvira's mind; she couldn't think why. She picked up the can of macaroni, the pan, and the spoon, and put them away. She wasn't hungry anymore.

9

Little by little, the explosions slowed down inside Elvira's brain, and a merciful numbness wrapped itself around her. For no particular reason she could name, she went outside and started walking. After a while, she found herself on the hill. She hadn't really meant to go there, but it didn't matter; nothing mattered—it was as good a place as any. She sat down beside the ant bed. The ants were scurrying about importantly.

"I didn't bring y'all nothin' today," she told them. "I forgot. I guess you didn't pray hard enough."

The ants didn't seem to notice, anyway. She wondered dully if they had ever noticed her. Probably not. They didn't know anything; they didn't care about anything. They were lucky.

She stared out at the highway. The heat was making the air shimmer, the way it does in a movie when someone is supposed to be dreaming . . .

She had always had vivid dreams—so vivid that sometimes she couldn't tell if something had really happened or if she had dreamed it. Her earliest memory was of a morning when she was very young—younger than five, anyway, because her mother had still been alive. She had awakened early, before her parents were up, and walked outside—the trailer door was never locked. And there, scattered all around in the dirt and gravel and occasional clumps of grass, were the bodies of maybe a hundred little snakes, all of them with their throats cut wide open. She had stood there, staring, not really frightened—they were dead, after all—but puzzled. And then she had walked back into the trailer; her mother was just getting out of bed. "Mama," she had asked, "what's all them dead snakes doin' outside?"

Her mother had smiled serenely. "Why, darlin', your daddy killed those snakes in the night. They were tryin' to get us, but he wouldn't let them. Now, hush—don't wake him; he's tired out from all that hard work . . ."

Elvira had suddenly felt tired, too, and had gone back to bed. She would think about that morning sometimes and feel glad that her daddy wouldn't ever let anything get her, but she never mentioned it again, until the day of her mother's funeral. It had come back into her mind then, and this time, for some reason, it had seemed important to talk about it.

"Daddy," she had whispered, tugging on his coat sleeve (she couldn't remember ever seeing him in a coat and tie, except for that one time—it made him look stiff and strange). "Daddy, do you 'member the time you killed all those snakes? Musta been a hunderd of 'em."

But Hank had looked down at her with eyes that didn't really see her. "Hush up, Elvira," he had said. "I never killed no snakes. Now, you keep still."

That was how she had found out that it had been a dream . . .

She wondered now if someday she might find out that this day was no more than a dream, too. "Daddy," she'd say, "do you 'member the time you said that I was gonna hafta go live with Aunt Darla?"

"What are you talkin' about, Elvira?" he'd say. "I never said no such thing. You musta been dreamin' again . . ."

No. There was no use in thinking that way. Not a bit of use. Aunt Darla was hardly the stuff dreams are made of—nightmares, maybe—but this was no nightmare, either. Nightmares at least felt like something. This felt like nothing—nothing at all.

Elvira wondered vaguely if she ought to pray, but she doubted that it would do any good; she didn't figure that anybody would hear her, any more than she had ever heard those ants down in their hidden temples . . . Anyhow, she had never known anybody to actually get anything out of praying, unless she was supposed to believe that baloney about Noreen Able being best friends with the Holy Ghost . . . Besides, Elvira didn't know any prayers but the "Now I Lay Me," and that didn't seem particularly appropriate right now . . .

A bird started singing somewhere close by.

"Shut up," she told it. "I got to think."

The bird went right on singing. Elvira lay down on her back and stared up at the sky. It was high and blue . . . blue and high . . . Friends in high places—Hank had said something about friends in high places . . . That's what I need me, thought Elvira—a friend in a high place . . . Maybe ol' Noreen had the right idea, after all. You'd have to look pretty hard to find a friend in a place any higher up than that . . .

That fool bird was still singing. Elvira spotted it in the branches of a spindly little sweet gum tree. It was a beady-eyed, potbellied mockingbird, just as fat and sassy as Aunt Darla . . . Elvira sat up and glared at it.

"I won't go," she said out loud. "I just flat won't go. They cain't make me." Just saying it made her feel better, so she said it again. "You hear me?" she hollered at the mockingbird. "I said they cain't make me go!"

The bird stopped singing, eyed her disapprovingly, and flew away.

Elvira's brain was working again. It was as if her defiant words were magic—they had opened a door somewhere deep inside her head, and the goo started oozing out . . . *The Blob* was beginning to disintegrate . . .

She had to think. She had to think. The end of August was still three weeks away. Maybe there was still some way to get Hank to change his mind—not that Hank had much of a history of changing his mind about anything; he was hardheaded as all get-out. But there had to be a way this time. There just had to be. Because Elvira wasn't going to Aunt Darla's. Not ever. She had decided.

She had to think. There wasn't any use in arguing

with Hank about it; she knew that. Arguing would only make him more dead-set on it than ever. What she needed was a plan—an inspiration . . . She thought again of Noreen Able and how she had claimed to have a corner on the inspiration market. Elvira knew it was nothing but blabber, but she couldn't help wishing now that it had been true. Noreen had never won any prizes for brains; if she could get inspired, well, then maybe Elvira could, too . . . She knew it was silly, but she whispered a quick "Now I Lay Me," just for luck . . .

She had to think. She had to think.

For the next few days, Elvira did nothing but think. She thought so hard her brain ached; it raced around like A. J. Foyt at the Indy 500—round and round and round again. It wouldn't stop even when she lay in bed at night—only half of her would go to sleep—the other half was thinking, thinking, thinking . . .

She thought up a thousand different plans and threw them out as fast as she thought them. She thought about all the old movies and television shows she had ever seen; she searched in every corner of her memory for a plot that might give her an idea. But she couldn't think of a one that would do her any good; as far as she could remember, every time things went wrong for kids on television, the kids would just run away.

That wouldn't help her any; she didn't want to run away—she wanted to stay right where she was. That was the whole point, wasn't it? Sure it was.

Friday came and went, and so did Saturday and Sunday, and still she was no closer to thinking of a plan. But the certainty inside her was growing steelier by the minute—she couldn't go, she wouldn't go . . .

And then, on Monday morning, the answer came. It was as clear as a bell ringing—or a telephone ringing—the pay phone outside of the trailer court office; Hank and Elvira didn't have their own private phone . . .

Hank was out that morning, talking to somebody at the Steinman Arms about a job as a night watchman. Elvira was sitting at the kitchen table, making a list in her spiral notebook. She was big on lists. She had learned that from Mrs. D. W. LeBlanc, who had taught her the second half of fifth grade back in Silsbee. Mrs. LeBlanc used to say, "When in doubt, make a list." Elvira was, so she did:

THINGS I MIGHT DO:

1. *Write the police an anonamous letter saying that Aunt Darla and Uncle Roy are communist spies.*
   Good side—They might go to jail.
   Bad side—They might not. And even if they do, when they get out, they will still come get me.

2. *Tell Hank that I will die if he makes me go.*
   Good side—This is the truth.
   Bad side—He probly would not beleave me.
3. *Go on to Sulfer Springs and when I get there act like that girl in* The Exersist.
   Good side—They will get rid of me in nothing flat.
   Bad side—They might send me to Rusk and lock me up in the insane asilem.
4. *Last rezort. Run away.*
   Good side—I wouldn't have to go to Aunt Darla's.
   Bad side—Where would I go? Plus of, who would water my garden while I went there?

Elvira was biting on the end of her ballpoint pen and trying to think of a number five when somebody knocked on the trailer door. She jumped up; her first thought was that Hank had accidentally locked himself out—hardly anybody else ever came to their door.

But it wasn't Hank. It was the tall, skinny man who worked in the office.

"You got a phone call," said the man. Elvira didn't even know his name.

"My daddy ain't in right now."

"Not your daddy—you. You're Elvira Trumbull, right?"

"Yessir."

"Well, come on, then. And tell whoever it is to make it snappy. That phone oughtn't to be tied up."

He didn't sound any too friendly, but Elvira didn't waste any time worrying about him; there wasn't anything worth noticing about him, anyway, except for maybe his Adam's apple, which happened to be the largest Elvira had ever seen on a human being . . . Her thoughts were all trained on that phone call—who in the world would be calling her? She ran all the way to the pay phone, so that she was out of breath when she answered.

"H-hello?"

"Elvira, is that you? This is Ivy Alexander."

Elvira's heart gave a glad little leap. "Yes, ma'am, it's me."

"Well, how are you, sweetheart? We haven't seen you in a few days."

"I'm just fine . . ." This was close enough to the truth; she was all right now that she had decided she wouldn't be going to Aunt Darla's. Her brain was just tired out from thinking so much, that was all.

"Well, that's good. And how's your garden coming along?"

"It's doin' all right, I think—I'm doin' like you told me about the water and everything."

"Good girl. I knew you would. I'll tell you why I called, Elvira. I was just wondering if you might be able to do me a little favor?"

"Yes, ma'am, I'd be glad to," answered Elvira, without hesitation. She would have done a lot more than a little favor for Miss Ivy.

Miss Ivy laughed. "Well, that's awfully nice of you, Elvira, but wait a minute—you haven't heard what it is yet."

"That's all right. It don't matter what it is. I'll do it."

"Thank you, sweetheart. I really appreciate that. But don't worry—this isn't anything too hard. I was just hoping that you might be able to spend some time with the boys this afternoon and then maybe stay for dinner this evening. Do you think you could do that?"

"Well, sure, Miss Ivy, but—but that ain't no favor . . ."

"Oh, yes, it is. You see, I'm afraid the boys are feeling sort of low today, and I thought maybe you could cheer them up a little."

"Are they sick?"

"No, no, not a bit. They're just disappointed—it's their father who's sick. He called early this morning. You know, today was the day he was supposed to come pick them up and take them over to Houston with him, and they've really been counting on it. But it looks as if their trip will have to be postponed indefinitely now—until he's well and can get some more time off." There was just a hint of irritation in Miss Ivy's voice. Elvira wondered if the boys' daddy was really sick; somehow, she doubted it . . . I knew he was no-account, she told herself. I knew it all along. Poor old Curtis—I bet he's takin' it hard . . .

Aloud she said, "Well, I'll be glad to go see 'em."

"Oh, good; that's so nice of you. I just hated it that I had to go to work today. Of course, Mrs. McFaddin is there with them, but I'd feel so much better knowing that they had you there, too."

Elvira tingled with pride. Did Miss Ivy think as much of her as all that? "What time should I go over?" she asked.

"Whatever's convenient for you. I surely do appreciate it, Elvira. I've got to run now—people are starting to come in—but I'll see you at suppertime, all right?"

"Yes, ma'am."

"Thanks again. 'Bye, Elvira."

" 'Bye, Miss Ivy."

Elvira hung up the receiver and started walking back to the trailer. She felt better than she had felt since Hank had broken the news about Aunt Darla; talking to Miss Ivy always made her feel better. She was such a nice lady—it was a real shame that she had married someone so jerkified . . . Elvira wondered if she'd ever get married again. It might be nice for those boys if she did . . .

It was then that it hit her. The inspiration. Pure-D inspiration—manna from heaven—the Holy Ghost

Himself, maybe . . . Whatever it was, it hit her so hard that she almost fell down right there in front of the man with the Adam's apple, who was standing in the doorway of the trailer park office, blowing smoke rings. Elvira started trembling all over. Her heart was beating a mile a minute. Her eyebrows began to sweat. She wouldn't have been all that surprised if she had started speaking in tongues.

She managed, somehow, to get back to the trailer. Then her legs wouldn't hold her up anymore, so she sat down shakily in the dirt beside her garden, closed her eyes, and breathed a fervent prayer: "Dear God, I take back everything I ever said about Noreen Able . . ."

10

It was all so simple, really. The simplest thing in the world . . .

All she had to do was introduce Miss Ivy to Hank. Once he met her, he'd be sure to fall in love with her—he couldn't help it—nobody could. And then they wouldn't need Aunt Darla anymore; what Hank had said about Aunt Darla being family and the Trumbulls not needing any outsiders—well, what if Miss

Ivy was family? What if Hank and Miss Ivy were to get married? She'd be family then! Oh, yes, it was the answer to everything, for everybody . . .

Hank would be happy. Elvira was sure of that. And it would be good for Miss Ivy, too. A lady pretty as she was ought to have a husband to look out for her and be nice to her, and Hank could be nice as pie when he was in a good mood. And he wasn't bad-looking, either—Elvira had never given it much thought before, but it was important now—well, sure, he wasn't bad-looking at all. He'd be kind of a John Wayne type if he just lost a little weight . . . And those boys needed a daddy—no question about that. That old guy in Houston didn't count for much, as far as Elvira could tell . . . And as for Elvira herself— Well. The thought of having Miss Ivy for a mother was so sweet that it almost hurt to think it.

She just had to figure some way to get them together. That shouldn't be too hard . . . She'd ask Miss Ivy over to dinner—that's what she'd do. A real romantic dinner with candlelight and all, like she'd seen in those magazines over at the U-Totem. She wouldn't ask Hank if it was all right; she'd just do it, and then tell him about it when it was too late for him to say no. It was for his own good—he'd thank her for it later on, even if he hollered about it at the time . . . There was the question of money, of course, but she could work that out—Hank had tired of doing all the grocery shopping and was trusting it to her again sometimes. Oh, she could do it—she really could—and if she got Hank and Miss Ivy off on the right foot, well, then, everything else would just naturally fall into place. It had to.

Elvira's head was still spinning. Come on now, girl, she told herself—you ain't got time to faint and fall out—you got things to do . . . She pulled herself up on her feet and went inside the trailer. It was lunchtime, but she couldn't eat a bite. She was full already—full to overflowing—it felt as if she had swallowed the sun. It crossed her mind that the Holy Ghost must have an awful lot of thin friends . . . Anyway, she figured that she ought to be getting over to Miss Ivy's pretty soon. She washed her face and hands and was about to go back outside when Hank got home. He looked worn out. He hadn't been looking too good for the last few days, as a matter of fact, and he was quieter than ever. Elvira hadn't really paid it any mind before, but now it worried her; she was going to have to think of some way to spruce him up for the dinner party . . .

"You fixin' to go somewhere?" he asked her, as he sat down wearily at the kitchen table. Every movement seemed to cost him a great effort.

"Yessir."

"Well, where you off to?"

"Miss Ivy's. She asked me to go play with her little boys. I'm s'posed to stay for supper."

Hank lifted his head and looked as if this was somehow surprising, but when he spoke, his voice was flat and tired sounding. "You never told me she had kids."

"I didn't? Well, I meant to—I guess I just never thought of it," said Elvira. "They're—they're real nice boys," she added, as an afterthought. It couldn't hurt to get started on her campaign right away. "Their daddy lives over in Houston. Miss Ivy and him's divorced. That's too bad, ain't it?"

"Hmmm?" Hank didn't seem to be paying good attention.

"I said Miss Ivy's divorced—ain't that too bad?"

"Oh, I don't know—I guess . . ."

Hank appeared to be done talking, so Elvira moved toward the door again. "Well, 'bye," she said.

"Elvira," he called to her when she was halfway out.

"Yessir?" she answered, coming back in again.

"Are you feelin' all right about—well, are you feelin' all right now?"

Elvira reddened. She knew what he meant. He meant had she gotten used to the idea of going to Aunt Darla's. Well, the truth was, she really was feeling just fine now—a little trembly, still, but it was a good kind of trembly. But there was no way she could explain to him that the reason was that she knew she wouldn't be going to Aunt Darla's; no way she could explain that now—not yet. So all she said was, "Yessir, I—I feel all right."

"Well. That's good—that's real good. You go on now."

Hank watched her run outside. She really did look like she was feeling better today; she looked—right pert, he thought. He figured that she must have thought it over and seen that she'd be a lot better off without her crotchety old man. She's got a lot more sense than I give her credit for, Hank told himself.

But somehow, this didn't make him feel as glad as it ought to have; all he felt was a kind of dull ache . . . Probably just some kind of acid in my stomach, he decided. Been drinkin' too much coffee lately . . .

If Elvira hadn't been all of eleven years old, she would have skipped the whole way to Miss Ivy's. She felt that good. Let's see now, she thought. This is Monday . . . If Miss Ivy comes over on, say, Friday night, that'd still leave two weeks before Aunt Darla's s'posed to get here . . . How long does it take for people to fall in love, anyhow? It don't usually take more than a half hour on television . . . I guess two weeks ought to be plenty long enough.

Curtis and John David were sitting out in the front yard when Elvira got to Miss Ivy's. A rush of affection swept over Elvira when she saw them; they were going to be her little brothers someday. But it didn't seem as if they were all that overjoyed to see her. They looked as dismal as the day after Christmas.

"Hi, boys—how're y'all doin'?" Elvira called out cheerfully.

"Terrible," said John David. John David hadn't yet learned how to lie.

"Aw, we're all right," said Curtis, who had. "He's just in a bad mood."

"Whatd'ya mean *I'm* in a bad mood?" cried John David. "*You're* in a badder mood than me—you're in the baddest mood I ever saw!" He turned sorrowfully to Elvira. "It's 'cause we didn't get to go to Astroworld. Our daddy won't take us."

"Will you just shut up, John David?" exploded Curtis. "That's not anybody else's business. And anyhow, it's not that Daddy *won't* take us—he just *can't* take us, that's all. He's sick—he can't help that."

Sure, thought Elvira. I'll bet. But aloud she said, "Well, what are we gonna do this afternoon, anyway? I came over to play with y'all."

Elvira thought she heard Curtis mutter something that sounded suspiciously like "Who cares?" but she chose to ignore this. If she was going to be a big sister, she might as well do it right and not start off by fighting.

"We could play Voltron," said John David hopefully. He looked as if he had had just about enough of being depressed.

"I'm sick of Voltron," said Curtis.

"Well, what about Orcs and Mighty Warriors?" suggested John David. "You can be a Mighty Warrior, if you want to, and Elvira and me'll be the Orcs . . ."

"I'm sick of that, too," Curtis said. "I'm sick of everything."

"Aw, c'mon, Curtis," said Elvira, "you really are in a bad mood. I'll tell you what we can do—I'll go set up the sprinkler and y'all can get on your bathing suits and run around in the water—what about that?"

"Oh, yeah, that'd be great!" cried John David. "Wouldn't that be great, Curtis?" He looked anxiously at his brother.

Curtis shrugged his shoulders. The others took this for a positive sign, all things considered, and in a little while the boys were laughing and shrieking and having the time of their lives . . .

When they finally tired of running around in the water, Elvira turned off the sprinkler, and they all spread towels on the grass and lay down in the sun.

"You ever been to Astroworld, Elvira?" Curtis asked quietly, after a while. He didn't sound so dismal anymore—just thoughtful.

"Uh-uh," said Elvira. "My daddy and me—we just never got around to it." She glanced sideways at Curtis and then went on, in an off-handed manner, "I expect we will sometime, though. My daddy takes me a lot of places."

"It's really fine over there," Curtis continued, in the same dreamy tone. "They got this roller coaster called the Texas Cylone. There's this man who's supposed to know all about roller coasters—that's all he does—travels around the world going from one roller coaster to another. And he says the Texas Cyclone is the best one of all."

"I might be tall enough to ride it this year," said John David. "I was almost tall enough last year, and I've growed a whole bunch since then."

"Aw, John David—you were tall enough last year, don't you remember? You were just too scared."

"I wasn't either scared—I really wanted to ride it; my head didn't come up to that cardboard cowboy's hand, that's all."

"All right, all right, if you say so," said Curtis, rolling his eyes at Elvira. He was silent for a while. Then he turned over on his stomach and propped himself up on his elbows. "You know there were two people who got married on a roller coaster one time?"

"Naw . . ."

"I swear—they had their picture in the paper and everything—my daddy cut it out. He likes roller coasters a whole lot, too. You shoulda seen it—the bride's veil was flyin' out in back of her, and the preacher was sittin' backward on the seat in front of her and the groom—it was really neat."

"Sounds crazy to me," said Elvira, but she smiled and tried to imagine Hank and Miss Ivy on that roller coaster . . .

"I think I'll get married on a roller coaster," said John David. "I mean, when I'm tall enough," he added hastily.

"Not me," said Curtis. "I'd like the roller coaster part all right, but I'm not ever gettin' married."

"You might change your mind someday," said Elvira. "I mean, if you found the right person . . ."

"Not me," Curtis insisted. "Not ever. No way."

Everybody was quiet again for a few minutes. Elvira was trying to decide if this would be a good time to start easing the boys into her plan . . .

"You know," she began tentatively, after a minute or two had passed, "your mama might get married again someday—maybe to somebody real nice."

"Like who?" said Curtis, a little belligerently.

"Oh, I don't know—just somebody . . ."

"I hope it's somebody real, *real* nice," said John David, "somebody who'll take us to Disneyland and buy me a horse."

"There ain't nobody *that* nice," Elvira said. "Anyhow, that ain't just nice—that's rich."

"Well, it'd be okay if he was rich," said John David.

"Aw, John David, you don't know what you're talkin' about," said Curtis. "We don't want Mama gettin' married again—that's nothin' but trouble. You just don't remember."

"I do too remember—why are you always sayin' I don't remember? I remember just as good as you do. I remember the time Mama threw the tomato and everything . . ."

"You don't tell stuff like that," Curtis said. "That's private."

"I can tell what I want, Curtis Alexander—you're not the boss of me. It was real funny, Elvira—Mama got real mad at Daddy and she threw this big old tomato at him and it splatted all over the kitchen and then they got divorced."

"You know, John David, you got a big mouth for a little kid," his brother informed him darkly.

"I'm not little," said John David, with dignity. "I'm just short."

The rest of the afternoon passed comfortably. Elvira avoided any further mention of the possibility of Miss Ivy's remarriage, and the boys seemed to forget all about it. They're just not ready to think about it yet, Elvira decided. But they'll come around . . .

The three of them were in the front yard playing Swing the Statue when Miss Ivy's car pulled into the driveway.

"Hello, everybody—have you all had a good day?" she called as she climbed out.

The boys ran to meet her, but Elvira held back, a little shyly. She was looking at Miss Ivy with brand-new eyes. She had thought her pretty before, but now she could see that she was more than pretty—she was perfect. Absolutely perfect, no matter how many tomatoes she had thrown at her no-account husband . . .

Elvira waited until she thought the moment was just right to invite Miss Ivy over for Friday night. The supper things had all been cleared away, and the boys had disappeared somewhere in the back of the house.

"Well, I guess we'd better be getting you home," Miss Ivy was saying. "It must be late."

"Uh, Miss Ivy," Elvira began, with her heart in her mouth, "I was just wonderin'—I mean, me and my daddy—we was both wonderin'—if you could come over to the trailer for dinner this Friday."

Miss Ivy looked surprised. "Well, that's awfully nice of you—but, sweetheart, you don't owe me a dinner . . ."

"No, ma'am, it ain't that . . . We—we really would like for you to come—my daddy and me—we're both countin' on it . . . It ain't no trouble atall—I got it all planned out." She looked up earnestly at Miss Ivy.

"Well, then, of course I'll come," said Miss Ivy, smiling. "I'd be honored."

Elvira breathed a sigh of relief. "Oh, good—I'm real glad. I'm sorry we cain't ask the boys this time . . . the trailer's kind of small . . ."

She wanted Hank to see Miss Ivy all by herself, this first time, so that he'd get the full impact. He could meet the boys another time, she figured. Friday night, there couldn't be any spilt milk or little kids' arguments clouding up the picture. Friday night, everything had to be *perfect*.

11

There was so much to do . . .

Elvira spent all of Tuesday morning sitting cross-legged on the floor in front of the magazine rack at the U-Totem, poring over every magazine that had a food section. She had to find the ideal menu for the dinner party—something delicious and exciting and unforgettable and cheap. Cheap, mainly. That pretty well eliminated some of her first choices—"crown roast of lamb" and "brandied steak" and "roast loin of pork St. Cloud"—Elvira loved the sound of that last one, especially—"St. Cloud". . . But she had seen the meat prices at Kroger. Hamburger Helper was more her speed . . .

She was just about to give up on a magazine called *Kitchens of America* when she came to a page with the headline: NEED A LITTLE ROMANCE IN YOUR LIFE? LUIGI INVITES YOU TO ITALY FOR THE EVENING! Under the words was a big color picture of a beautiful woman and a handsome man at a table for two—it looked as if they were floating in the air in front of some Italian city or other. Their eyes were sparkling in the candlelight . . . There was a checkered tablecloth on the table and a crystal vase filled with roses and long-stemmed wine glasses half-filled with ruby-red wine and gilt-edged dinner plates piled high with spaghetti . . .

It was just an ad for Luigi's Spaghetti Sauce. That was all. But Elvira knew right away that it was perfect—that man and that woman were looking at each other just the way she wanted Miss Ivy and Hank to look at each other. And spaghetti was just the thing, too; it was tasty, it wasn't too hard to fix, it was cheap—it was perfect. Another inspiration.

Elvira looked at the picture for a long time, trying

to memorize every detail . . . spaghetti and bread and salad and wine and . . . what about dessert? They had to have dessert, didn't they? Elvira laid down *Kitchens of America*—carefully, so as not to lose the magic picture—and thumbed through three more magazines before she found the answer. It was another picture—a picture of a lemon meringue pie—so lovely and luscious looking that it almost brought tears to her eyes. CREATE THE ULTIMATE DESSERT, said the caption. IT'S SIMPLE WITH CARLSON CORNSTARCH. The ultimate dessert. Well. That was the one, all right.

Elvira couldn't afford to buy the magazines, but she had brought along her spiral notebook, so she copied down the recipe for the pie and made notes about the spaghetti ad—"Checkered tablecloth, drippy candle stuck in fat bottle, salid, Italyun bread, roses . . ."

Oh, it was going to be a wonderful dinner—a beautiful dinner—a perfect dinner!

She spent the afternoon at Kroger, finding out how much everything was going to cost. She made a list and added it up:

Ground beef (1 pound)	—	$1.49
Spagetty (1 box)	—	.59
Luigi's Sp. Sauce	—	2.29
Italyun bread	—	1.19
Lemons (4 for)	—	1.00
Cornstarch	—	.47

Lettuce	—	.89
Salid dressing	—	1.05
Candle	—	.99
		$9.96

Nine dollars and ninety-six cents! And not even counting the tax! That was cutting it pretty close; Hank didn't usually give her more than ten dollars at a time, and she'd probably have to get milk or bread or something like that, besides. Well, he'd have to give her a couple of dollars extra this time. He'd just have to.

Elvira spent all of Wednesday cleaning the trailer. She dusted it and swept it and squirted so much EZ-Kleen everywhere that the whole place reeked of ammonia . . .

"What in the heck's that smell?" asked Hank, when he came home from job-hunting that afternoon.

"Oh, I just felt like doin' a little housecleanin'," answered Elvira, wishing her face wouldn't get so red. "It—it don't really smell all that strong, does it?" she added anxiously. She didn't want Miss Ivy thinking the trailer smelled peculiar . . .

Fortunately, the smell had pretty much worn away by Thursday. Thursday was shopping day.

"Uh, I was just wonderin'," Elvira began, when Hank had finished his coffee that morning—there wouldn't have been any use in her asking him anything until he had his coffee— "I was just wonderin'—

we're gettin' pretty low on groceries—maybe I could run over to Kroger and pick up a couple of things—would that be all right?"

"Hmmm?" Hank was staring off into space; he seemed to be about a million miles away.

"Groceries, I said—we need some groceries. I could go over there right now . . ."

"Oh, all right," said Hank absently. "I guess we do need some things." He pulled out his old, beat-up wallet—smashed flat by long years of being sat on without having much inside—got out two five-dollar bills, and handed them to Elvira.

She took a deep breath. "Uh, I need a little more than that—just a couple dollars more."

Hank looked at her. "You ain't thinkin' 'bout buyin' another one of them rosebushes?" he asked. He didn't really sound mad—just tired.

"Oh, no, sir—just groceries—I swear."

"Girls oughtn't to swear," said Hank, but to Elvira's huge relief, he pulled out another two dollars . . .

Elvira did all the shopping that morning and spent the rest of the day working on decorations. She stuck the candle she had bought into an empty ketchup bottle covered with tin foil, cut up an old sheet to use as a tablecloth, and made a half-dozen roses out of Kleenex, since her poor old rosebush was fresh out; fortunately, Miss Reba Foxworth had taught the fourth graders in Angleton everything there was to know about Kleenex roses . . . Well, thought Elvira when she was done, it don't look all that much like the magazine picture, but I bet it won't be half bad by candlelight.

There was still the problem of telling Hank about the dinner party. Elvira decided that she was going to have to do it tonight—tomorrow was Friday; she really couldn't put it off any longer. She rehearsed the whole conversation carefully in her mind. She went over it and over it, so she'd be sure to say all the right things . . .

Hank got home just before dark. They had chili and crackers for supper; Elvira had worked a can of chili into her purchases, so Hank wouldn't ask her how she had managed to spend twelve dollars on groceries and not get anything for supper. His mood seemed to have improved some; he talked a little while they ate.

"I was over at Kinsel Automotive this afternoon. They said come back next week—I might be able to fill in for a guy who's goin' on vacation."

"That's good," said Elvira. Inside her head she said, All right, go ahead and tell him now—this is the time to tell him, while he's feelin' pretty good . . .

She tried to make her voice sound normal. "Uh, there's somethin' I been meanin' to tell you about—I mean, ask you about."

"Well, what is it?" Hank looked right at her; it

made her pretty nervous, but she forced herself to keep talking.

"It's all right, ain't it—if—if Miss Ivy comes over here to dinner tomorrow night?" Elvira tried to make it sound like nothing at all—just a casual kind of thing, as if they had guests for dinner every night.

But Hank didn't take it quite that lightly. "You mean, that—woman?" He might as well have said, "You mean, that—alligator?" for the tone he said it in.

"Y-yessir, you know—my friend—Miss Ivy . . ."

Hank pushed his chair back from the table. "Good Lord, Elvira—I don't want some woman comin' over here for dinner—what are we gonna give her—half a can of tuna fish? We're doin' well just to feed ourselfs, as it is."

Elvira was ready for that; it was just what she had counted on him saying. "I got that all worked out," she said, her confidence growing as she recited her lines. "I thought we'd have spaghetti tomorrow night—it's real cheap, you know, and I already got everything I need for it—there's plenty for three people."

But Hank just shook his head. "For two people, you mean. You and your friend. I guess she can come over, if you really want her to that bad, but y'all don't need me here. I don't want to be sittin' around tryin' to think of somethin' to say to some—woman."

"But—" Elvira was thrown for a loop; her voice lost its confidence. "But, you got to be here . . ."

"Why? She's your friend, not mine—she don't care nothin' about seein' me."

"But I already told Miss Ivy you'd be here, and she wants to meet you—"

"No, she don't. She's just sayin' that to be nice; women are always sayin' things they don't mean. I'm tellin' you, your friend don't want to be botherin' with me any more than I want to be botherin' with her."

Elvira was silent for a moment. She had to think—there had to be some way to get Hank to come to the dinner . . . Funny, she had thought that the hard part would be getting him to agree to let Miss Ivy come, not in getting him to show up himself . . .

"But it's—it's s'posed to be sorta like a party," she faltered. "You know—a real party—for you and me and Miss Ivy—I got it all planned out . . ."

"What do you mean, a party? What is it, her birthday or somethin'?"

Elvira turned red. She looked down at her crackers. "No, sir, it ain't nobody's birthday."

"Well, then, why . . ." began Hank, and then he broke off suddenly. He stared at Elvira for a moment. Then he stood up and began pacing around the little kitchen like an old bear in a cage, mumbling to himself . . . Elvira caught the words "memory of a fence post . . ." After a couple of minutes of this, he stopped and leaned on the sink; he turned on the water for no apparent reason and then turned it off once more. When he spoke again, his voice was different—quieter—

"I forgot your birthday, didn't I? You turned eleven the end of July . . ." He didn't look at her; he just kept staring into the sink.

"It don't matter," said Elvira nervously. "It's just little kids who care about that kinda thing. I'm—I'm way too old for that now."

"You wouldn't catch Darla forgettin' a thing like that," muttered Hank.

Elvira wished he hadn't thought of the birthday; now he'd be in a bad mood and never agree to come to dinner . . .

He didn't say he was sorry. Hank was never any good at saying he was sorry. Instead, he said, "For Gordon's seed, Elvira, why didn't you tell me? You should have told me."

Now Elvira felt guilty; it was her fault, somehow. If everything was ruined it would be all her own fault. She didn't say anything. She couldn't think of anything else to say.

Hank turned around from the sink, but he still didn't look directly at Elvira. He seemed to be concentrating on scratching a little glob of dried chili off the stove with his fingernail . . .

"What time's your—your friend s'posed to get here, anyway?"

Elvira looked up, hardly daring to hope. "Eight o'clock."

"All right, then, eight o'clock," said Hank uncomfortably. "I don't guess there's nothin' else I got to be doin' tomorrow night at eight o'clock."

Elvira was so relieved she could have hugged him, but Hank wasn't much on hugging; that sort of thing embarrassed him. So she just folded her arms tightly across her chest and tried to hold in her gladness . . . Everything was going to work out all right, after all. And eight o'clock tomorrow night was barely twenty-four hours away.

12

Elvira woke up the next morning in a cold sweat. She had dreamed she was in Oz—only it was really the Calder Public Library—and she couldn't get home to fix dinner, because the Wicked Witch had changed her ruby slippers into overdue notices . . .

It was a dream, she told herself—just a dumb dream. Everything's gonna be just fine. Sure it is.

There was still so much to do. She had to settle

down and do it, one step at a time. Thank the Lord she had made herself another list last night. Mrs. D. W. LeBlanc would have been proud. Elvira climbed out of bed, got out her spiral notebook, and opened it.

THINGS I MUST DO ON FRIDAY:
1. Bake pie.

She stopped right there and closed her eyes. The thought of the pie was soothing to her soul. She could see it quite clearly, just the way it had looked in the picture, with those little curlicues of white tipped with golden brown floating on top of that sunny yellow filling . . . Oh, yes, the pie—the "ultimate dessert"—baking the pie would be the perfect way to start a perfect day.

She carried her notebook to the kitchen, turned to the page where she had copied down the recipe, and started piling all the ingredients on the table. Cornstarch, sugar, salt—check. Lemon juice, lemon rind, water—check. Three eggs, separated— Separated? Elvira wondered why they had to be separated. Well, if that's what the recipe said . . . She got three eggs out of the refrigerator and carefully cracked them into three separate cereal bowls. There. Three eggs, separated—check. This was going to be a breeze.

She was about to plunge on into the cooking instructions when Hank came into the kitchen.

"What's all this?" he asked, looking in bewilderment at all the stuff set out on the kitchen table.

"I'm bakin' a pie," said Elvira proudly.

"A pie? Where'd you learn how to bake a pie?" Hank sounded impressed.

"Oh, there ain't nothin' to it—you just follow the recipe, that's all. I copied it out of a magazine."

"Well, if that don't beat all . . . That's real smart of you, Elvira. You know, I ain't had a piece of homemade pie since . . . well, in a long time," he finished.

"I'll clean you up a spot on the table, so you can have your coffee . . ."

"No, don't bother with that—I can have coffee downtown somewhere. I got to be gettin' downtown, anyway. You, uh, you need any help with anything before I go?"

Elvira lifted her chin confidently. "No, sir. I got it all under control."

Hank looked relieved. "Well, all right. I guess I'll see you later on, then . . . You said eight o'clock, right?"

"Y-yessir, but"—Elvira groped for words that wouldn't make him mad—"but, well, maybe you could get here a little earlier, so you'd have some time to—well, you know—kinda get ready . . ."

To her huge relief, Hank grinned. "You want me to get slicked up for your friend, huh? You don't hafta worry—I won't shame you." He started out the door. "See you later."

" 'Bye," Elvira called after him, and then she turned back to her pie with renewed enthusiasm. Hank had seemed so pleased that she was baking a pie . . . Well, then, she'd bake a pie he'd never forget.

That was at 9:36 A.M.

By 10:42, she was feeling a shade less enthusiastic . . . Everything was just hunky-dory to begin with. She had to mix up the cornstarch and some sugar and salt and water and cook it until it turned into a kind of jelly—"thick enough to mound slightly when dropped from spoon." That part was just fine. No problem. But then came the Great Egg Mystery. "Beat three egg yolks with one-half cup sugar," said the recipe. Not the whites—just the yolks. Now, how am I s'posed to beat the yolks without beatin' the whites? wondered Elvira, screwing up her forehead and scanning the rest of the recipe for clues . . . The only other mention of eggs was in the meringue part—"Beat egg whites until foamy." Hmmm—egg *whites*—now, that was interesting. The recipe never mentioned yolks and whites in the same breath . . . Aha! "Three eggs, separated" must have meant yolk from white—not egg from egg . . . But solving that riddle was no trick at all compared to the actual job of getting the dad-blamed yolks away from those slimy whites. It took Elvira forty-five minutes, four bowls, three spoons, nine eggs, and untold grief, but she finally did it.

11:37. Elvira was starting to sweat. The top of the

filling was full of lumps, and the bottom was burned. It smelled something like the Goodyear plant on a bad day. Well, heck, she told herself—I'll just have to start over again—there ain't nothin' else for it . . .

12:58. The back of Elvira's neck was beginning to ache, but she didn't have time to think about that. She had to get this pie baked . . . She had finally finished with the filling and was ready to move on to the meringue, so she got out her mother's old electric mixer and plugged it in. Well. That old mixer did a lot of things. It sputtered, it spurted, it showered sparks—just about the only thing it didn't do was work. All right, then, declared Elvira, her mouth set in a line of grim determination—I'll beat the dang whites with my own dang arm. That's what I'll do.

She did. She beat them and beat them and beat them . . .

1:44. Elvira was reasonably certain that her arm was going to fall off, but it didn't, and, sure enough, those egg whites actually started to bear a faint resemblance to the meringue in the picture . . .

2:29. Just the crust to go. Elvira was tired, but cheerful. This ought to be the easiest part of all, she told herself. Why, crust ain't nothin' but dough, and dough ain't nothin' but flour and Crisco and a little salt and water, right?

Wrong. That dough was the stickiest, glueyist, orneriest stuff that ever was. It stuck to everything in sight—Elvira's hands, the bowl, the flour-sprinkled table . . .

3:08. Elvira had just about had it with all desserts, ultimate or otherwise. She got out her mother's old rolling pin, pressed it to her sweaty forehead, and prayed that it would remember its stuff, but it didn't do any good. If that rolling pin had ever known anything about pie crust, it had forgotten. It didn't have a clue. It just sat there and stuck to the dough—or the dough stuck to it—it didn't matter; it was a mess no matter how you looked at it . . . Elvira scraped the gook off the rolling pin and started over again, but it didn't get any better—it got worse, if anything. So she scraped it off a second time and tried again . . . and again . . . and again . . .

4:33. Elvira scraped it off one last time and flung the whole mess disgustedly back into the bowl. She was a wreck. A total wreck. She felt betrayed. Just when she needed Him the most, the Holy Ghost had left town. Elvira didn't feel one bit inspired; she didn't feel one bit sure of herself. All she felt was frustrated and mad. Mad, mostly. Too mad to give up. Too mad to let herself be beaten by a lemon pie. Somehow, everything seemed to have come down to that pie; she felt as if her whole plan depended on that treacherous lump of gluey gunk . . .

Her plan—but what good was that, anyway? She

must have been out of her mind to believe in anything so ridiculous—as nutty as Noreen Able . . .

She squared her shoulders and looked fiercely at the enemy in the big plastic bowl. Well, she wasn't going down without a fight. She had to try—even if her plan didn't have a snowball's chance in Corpus Christi, it was better to try than to just give up and sit around waiting for Aunt Darla to come get her. She might be all out of inspiration, but she could still grit her teeth and try.

I got to start over again, she told herself, breathing deeply and trying her best to stay calm. Just one more time. And this time I'll use more flour—that's all it needs, I bet—just a little more flour . . .

When Hank walked into the kitchen at 5:45, a sorry sight met his eyes. The whole room was covered in flour—an inch deep in some places—more in the drifts. Elvira was collapsed in a chair. She looked like a ghost—a glassy-eyed ghost. She was snowy white from her nose to her toes.

"Good Lord-a-mercy, what happened in here?" yelled Hank, staring openmouthed at the mess.

"I did it," said Elvira wearily. "I baked a pie." She pointed to the table. There was a pie there, all right. A genuine, homemade, lemon meringue pie, just like the one in the magazine. It had nearly killed her, but there it was.

13

"Well, I'll swanny," said Hank, in a softer voice. "I'll swanny . . . that sure does look like one heck of a pie, all right."

"One heck of a pie," repeated Elvira stupidly. She was too tired to think of words of her own.

"But, Elvira, do you realize what time it is? Your company's gonna be here in a couple of hours."

Elvira sat bolt upright. The words crashed in on

her dazed mind like a bucket of ice water. "A-a couple of hours? It cain't be that late . . ."

"It's a quarter of six."

"A quarter of six? A *quarter* of *six*? Oh Lordy, where's my list? I got to find my list!" And then she was on her feet and tearing around like a tornado—a white tornado, trailing clouds of floury smoke . . ."Oh, Lordy, how could it take anybody all day to bake a pie? That's crazy—oh, Lord, where in the heck's my list, anyway . . ."

"This it here?" asked Hank, holding out the notebook, which had been lying on the table directly in front of her nose.

"That's it!" cried Elvira, grabbing the notebook and flipping it open to the right page. But her face fell again when she saw all it said . . .

> 2. *Fix spagetty sauce.*
> 3. *Fix salid.*
> 4. *Clean up kitchen.*
> 5. *Set table and dekrate.*
> 6. *Bathe and dress up.*
> 7. *Make sure Hank looks real nice.*
> 8. *Start water boiling for spagetty.*

"Oh, shoot, there ain't enough time—there just ain't enough time!" she wailed. She walked to one end of the kitchen and then changed her mind and walked to the other end. She picked up the broom, put it down, picked up the plastic bowl and started brushing flour into it, put that down, picked up the broom again, put that down one more time, walked to the refrigerator and started pulling stuff out, left and right . . .

For a moment, Hank just stood there, watching her. Then he started to chuckle. Elvira heard him; she wheeled around and looked at him. Her face was tight.

"What are you laughin' at?" she demanded. She was too upset to try to sound respectful.

Hank cleared his throat and made an effort to pull himself together, but there were still signs of laughter around his mouth and eyes. " 'Scuse me—I couldn't help it— For a minute there you just reminded me a whole lot of—somebody."

"You think this is f-funny?" cried Elvira, her eyes blazing. "Miss Ivy's gonna be here any minute . . . there ain't nothin' funny about it!"

Hank straightened his face out again. "No, it ain't a bit funny . . . Now, take it easy, Elvira. You just got you a case of the hostess panic—that's what we used to call it—I ain't seen such a bad case in a long time. Now, come on—settle down . . . Let me see that list you got there—maybe I can help you out some."

Hank was wonderful after that. Elvira couldn't get over how he pitched right in and helped out with everything. And somehow, it all got done—the sauce and the salad and the cleaning up and the setting of the table and the decorating, too, and there was still enough time left over for Hank to shave and Elvira to shower and both of them to get changed. Elvira put on a dress—her only dressy dress—the red and white one from that Christmas in Sulphur Springs; it was a little on the short side, but not all that much—she really hadn't grown a whole lot in the last two and a half years. And Hank combed his hair and put on a clean shirt and even a tie, at Elvira's request; she thought he looked just wonderful . . .

At a quarter of eight, they stood together in the kitchen, admiring the table. The plaid sheet made a fine tablecloth, and the ketchup bottle didn't look *too* much like a ketchup bottle, with the candle in it. It was a pretty candle—Elvira had chosen a nice shade of burnt orange to match the spaghetti sauce. The Kleenex roses weren't quite as professional looking as Miss Reba Foxworth's, but Elvira was counting on the candlelight to help there . . . She had told Miss Ivy eight o'clock especially so that it would be dark enough to light the candle . . .

"Seems to me like you're ready to go," said Hank. "It all looks just fine, don't it?"

"Yessir," said Elvira, " 'cept—well, it don't matter, I guess . . ."

"What don't matter?"

Elvira sighed. "The wine—there ought to be wine

on the table, in long-stemmed glasses . . . I forgot all about it, till now."

Hank rubbed his chin. "Elvira, we don't even know if this lady drinks, and if she does, well, I can offer her a beer."

Elvira shook her head. "No, sir, you cain't have beer with spaghetti—you got to have red wine." She couldn't quite put her feelings into words, but somehow she just couldn't imagine Miss Ivy drinking a beer; it didn't fit in the picture at all. But it was too late to worry about that now. They'd just have to do without the wine . . .

"I guess it don't really matter," she said. "You really think it looks all right?"

"It looks just fine. You've done a real nice job."

Elvira looked up at Hank and smiled. He was looking so handsome—all clean-shaven and neat; Elvira felt proud of him. Miss Ivy would like him. She would. She had to . . .

Hank looked down at Elvira, too, and then for just a second a kind of peculiar expression passed across his face . . .

"Uh, look, Elvira," he said suddenly, "I got to go someplace real quick—it won't take me but five minutes."

Elvira gave a little cry of alarm. "But—but you cain't leave now—Miss Ivy's due here any second!"

"Naw, you still got some time—it ain't even ten till

yet. And anyhow, women are most always late. I'll be right back." He hurried out the door . . .

Miss Ivy was late, just as Hank had said—five whole minutes late—but Hank still wasn't back when she arrived. Please make him come back, Elvira prayed, as she answered the knock. Please don't let him change his mind about comin' to the dinner—he's just got to come back . . ."

"Well, don't you look pretty tonight!" exclaimed Miss Ivy, when Elvira opened the trailer door.

"Thank you, ma'am—so do you," said Elvira. This was the truth. Miss Ivy had never looked lovelier. She was wearing white—angel white—a pretty cotton blouse with puffy sleeves and a flowing skirt of the same material. Her hair was brushed into reddish-gold waves that fell softly around her face, and her eyes were shining like twin pieces of the summer sky. She was holding a bouquet of flowers—all the loveliest ones from her garden . . .

"These are for my hostess," she said, putting them into Elvira's hands.

"Uh, thank you, ma'am," murmured Elvira. "They're sure pretty. You come on in and sit down—I'm gonna put these right on the table . . ." She rushed into the kitchen and whisked the Kleenex roses into the garbage before Miss Ivy had a chance to see them . . .

"Is there anything I can do to help you in here?" asked Miss Ivy, following her into the kitchen. "My goodness, you're so organized! And your table looks just beautiful."

It did look nice, especially with the real flowers—it was pretty near perfect. But what did it matter, if Hank wasn't there?

"Thank you, ma'am, but everything's done, 'cept for boilin' the noodles, and I cain't do that till the very last minute. Soon's my daddy gets back . . ." Elvira left off there, wondering how long she should wait before she gave up on him; she was beginning to have a kind of hopeless, sinking feeling in the pit of her stomach.

"Your father's not here?"

"No, ma'am. He—he had to go out for just a minute . . . Some—some kind of work, I expect—he's a—a real hard worker . . ."

"I'm sure he is," said Miss Ivy gently.

She's bound to think I'm lyin', thought Elvira. I got to do better than that . . . "It musta been an emergency, or he'da been right here—he's been countin' on meetin' you . . ." She don't believe a word I'm sayin', Elvira told herself. Shoot, I don't believe it myself. He don't want to come, that's all; he never wanted to come from the first minute I told him about it . . .

She hung her head in shame and disappointment. But just then there was the sound of tires screeching and a motor being shut off and a door slamming outside, and then the trailer door opened and Hank was there, holding a brown paper sack in one hand and looking ill at ease.

"I'm sorry to be late—I had a little trouble findin' a store that was still open . . ." He was looking at Elvira; Miss Ivy's back was toward the door. But then Miss Ivy turned around and smiled, and Elvira's heart started tap dancing in her chest. Because she had seen Hank's face. For just a second, it was the face of a little kid who has just seen Santa Claus and the tooth fairy and a genie out of a bottle all rolled into one. For just a second. Then it changed and got that strained, careful expression Hank always wore when he was talking to strangers. But Elvira had seen that first stunned, uncovered look, and now she knew she could hope again . . .

"You must be Miss Ivy," Hank was saying, in his most formal voice. "I'm Hank Trumbull—I'm mighty pleased to meet you."

Miss Ivy held out her hand. "I'm pleased to meet you, too, Mr. Trumbull."

"Call me Hank," he said, shifting the package to his left arm and shaking hands self-consciously. He handed the brown sack to Elvira. "This is for your dinner." He looked at Miss Ivy again. "Elvira says you cain't have spaghetti without red wine," he explained, grinning sheepishly.

Elvira gave a little gasp of gladness. "You got the

wine?" she cried, peering into the sack. There was a bottle of wine in there, all right, and a bottle of grape soda, and three things wrapped in tissue paper; she lifted them out—they were wine glasses—beautiful, long-stemmed wine glasses, just like in the picture. For some reason, sudden tears stung her eyes . . . She meant to say thank you, but all she could do was rush into the kitchen, mumbling, "I—I got to rinse these out . . ."

"Can I help?" Miss Ivy called after her.

"No—no, y'all stay in there and visit," said Elvira firmly, blinking hard. "I got everything under control . . ."

It was the nicest dinner anybody ever had. Nicer than the one in the magazine, even—with Miss Ivy's eyes shining in the candlelight, and the real flowers looking so lovely, and those elegant wine glasses half filled with ruby-red wine—Nehi grape for Elvira, but that was nice, too . . . Hank didn't talk all that much at first, but Elvira thought that was all right; she figured that he was too stunned by Miss Ivy to do much talking. And Miss Ivy—well, Miss Ivy was perfect. Just like Elvira had known she would be. She made the conversation flow as easily and naturally as running water—a kind of happy river of talk that carried the other two along with it effortlessly. She actually managed to get Hank to relax some and open up a little bit; he even told his stories about Noah Goode and the Hogg sisters, and Miss Ivy laughed as appreciatively as if he had been Johnny Carson or somebody like that. And all the while, Elvira just beamed on them both. They liked each other. They really did.

The food was good, too. The spaghetti tasted like real spaghetti, and the bread and salad were just fine; Elvira could hardly believe how well everything was going. She had only one more attack of nerves—when it was time to serve the pie. She had hidden it in her bedroom, so it would be a surprise for Miss Ivy; when she went to get it she whispered one last prayer to the Holy Ghost . . . "I'm sorry I quit believin' in you earlier today . . . Everything's goin' great . . . If you could just please see to it that this pie is all right, then I won't bother you for anything else—I'll take over from here . . ."

"A pie! Why, Elvira, you didn't make that yourself!" cried Miss Ivy, when Elvira carried it to the table.

"Yes, she did, too," Hank declared proudly. "Every bit of it."

Elvira blushed and hoped for the best. She cut three pieces, handed them out, and held her breath while Hank and Miss Ivy took their first bites . . .

Miss Ivy put down her fork and looked up solemnly. "Elvira," she said, "this is absolutely the best pie I ever put in my mouth."

"Mmm, mmm!" agreed Hank, his mouth full. "It's mighty good, daughter—mighty good."

Elvira smiled blissfully. The Holy Ghost had come through with flying colors . . .

I really appreciate it, she told Him, as she lay in her bed later that night, reliving every wonderful moment of the evening. But I guess I lied when I said I wouldn't ask you for anything else . . . There's gonna be a couple more things—just a couple more . . .

14

For the next few days, Elvira watched Hank impatiently for symptoms of lovesickness. But he wouldn't let on how he was feeling—if he was feeling anything. He has to be feeling something, Elvira told herself. She had seen the look in his eyes when he first saw Miss Ivy . . .

On Monday, he started filling in over at Kinsel Automotive. Elvira began to panic about the time;

there were only a couple of weeks left in August, and with Hank at work all day—even on Thursday, Miss Ivy's day off—there was hardly any time for her to get them together. She had to get them together again—that was all there was to it. The seed had been planted all right, but now it needed tending. But how?

It was John David who provided the answer, although he didn't mean to . . .

"I sure didn't mean to," he swore, for the fortieth time, while Curtis and Elvira stood by the television set at Miss Ivy's house, shaking their heads. Elvira had walked over to see the boys late Tuesday afternoon and found the household in turmoil. John David had dropped his Space Invaders' power magnet down the back of the TV, causing a minor explosion inside the set and a power failure in the rest of the house. The ice cream was melting in the freezer, the fans had stopped fanning, and the temperature was rising—not to mention the tempers.

"I don't know how anybody could be so dumb," said Curtis, also for the fortieth time. "How could you be so dumb, John David?"

"I *told* you I didn't mean to," said John David unhappily. "I was just holdin' it over that little crack in the back to see if it'd fit—I never meant to let go of it . . . It just sort of slipped out of my hand."

"Well, I tried to call Mrs. Alexander," said Mrs. McFaddin, coming in from the kitchen, where the phone was, "but they said she'd already left. I don't know that there's anything she can do, anyway; there's no way she's going to get a serviceman out here this late in the day."

"Oh, boy, John David, how could anybody do anything so dumb?" asked Curtis . . .

"I *told* you I didn't mean to!" wailed John David. "I told you and told you!"

"Well, I guess we just can't watch *The Bugs Bunny/Roadrunner Movie* that's on tonight, that's all."

"Oh, no!" groaned John David. "That's my best show!" This was too much. He crumpled up in a miserable heap on the floor and cried as if his heart would break.

Elvira knelt down beside him and patted his back. She was sorry for his trouble, but her own heart was suddenly light . . ."Don't cry, John David. I think I might know somebody who can fix it—maybe even before your show comes on."

"Wh-who?" hiccuped John David.

"My daddy," said Elvira, with pride. "He can fix televisions real good—one time he worked for a TV repair shop over in Silsbee. He's fixed ours before, too . . . I'll go call him right now."

Hank's voice was worried when he came on the line. "Elvira, are you all right?" She had never called him at any of his jobs before.

"Yessir, I'm just fine . . ."

"Well, good Lord, what is it, then? You had me scared to death—I thought there must be some emergency."

"Well, it is sort of an emergency. See, Miss Ivy's television is broke; her little boy put a magnet down the back of it . . ."

"A what?"

"A magnet—just a little magnet—but then their TV sort of exploded a little, and now all their electricity's gone out."

"Well, haven't they called somebody to come fix it?"

"Yessir, but everybody says it's too late today, and I was just thinkin' that maybe you could come by after work and take a look . . . They're havin' a real hard time . . ."

There was a moment's silence on the other end of the line. Elvira crossed her fingers. He's thinkin' about Miss Ivy now, she told herself. He's thinkin' about how pretty she is and how nice it would be to see her again and maybe help her out . . . Oh, come on, say you'll come, Hank . . .

"Well, I guess I could go over there for a little while," said Hank slowly. "Where is it she lives?"

When Elvira hung up the phone, she was so happy she could have kissed John David, but he had a lot of sticky, purple stuff on his face, so she thought better of it. Still, sticky or not, he had been an instrument of the Lord this day—that magnet hadn't slipped out of his hand entirely by accident—Elvira was sure of it.

Miss Ivy arrived first. John David met her at the front door. "You know what I made today, Mama?" he asked her, as he hugged her around the waist.

"I don't know—what did you make today, John David?" asked Miss Ivy, smiling at the others while she stroked his dark hair.

"A mistake," he said sorrowfully. And then the whole sad tale was told over again, and John David explained how he hadn't meant to do it, and Curtis offered his opinion on the subject and described the explosion in dramatic terms, and John David said that it hadn't been nearly as bad as that, and Mrs. McFaddin told her version, which was somewhere between the other two. And in the middle of all this, there was a knock on the front door. It was Hank.

"Elvira tells me y'all are havin' a little trouble over here," he said, when Miss Ivy opened the door. "I thought maybe I'd take a look."

"Oh, Mr. Trumbull, that's so nice of you!" Miss Ivy cried. Elvira wished she had remembered to call him Hank, but then that probably wasn't all that important; she figured she really couldn't complain about such a little detail, considering how well things were going.

Hank was a big hit that night. He did everything right. First, he disconnected the television. Then he found the breaker box in the utility room and got the electricity on again. Then he went back to the television, took it apart, removed the magnet, and put the set back together. Then, when it still didn't work, he took it apart a second time and fiddled and fumed and fooled with it until he finally got it going. And all the time he was working, John David was following him around respectfully, asking hard questions about wires and tubes and nuts and bolts, which Hank did his best to answer. Elvira felt so proud of him she could have popped. When he was done, Miss Ivy wanted to pay him, but he wouldn't hear of it; he said friends don't pay each other for helping out in a pinch. Elvira thought that about proved how much he liked her, as badly as he needed money . . . And then Miss Ivy wouldn't hear of the Trumbulls leaving without having supper first. Elvira could scarcely believe her good fortune.

They were eating hamburgers on the porch a little later when she suddenly shivered all over, in spite of the warm evening air. This was it—her family—sitting around the table having a quiet supper together . . . She felt so close to having her dream come true that she could almost taste it.

She looked at the way John David was watching Hank and imitating every move he made—the way he sat and leaned his chin on his hand and scratched the back of his neck every so often . . . John David even had his napkin tucked in under his chin, just the way Hank had his. John David was in the bag, Elvira could see that; he was already on her side, without even knowing it.

She looked at Curtis. Curtis was sitting next to his mother with a polite, but bored, expression on his face. Curtis wasn't going to be so easy; Curtis was always harder about everything. Ever since Hank had arrived, Curtis had kept his distance. He appeared to think it his duty to be tough and standoffish, to show how he could generally take care of things himself—he was the man of the house, after all.

I'm just gonna hafta do somethin' here, Elvira told herself—there ain't enough time left to sit around and hope things'll happen all by theirselfs . . .

"Hey, Curtis—you ever go fishin'?" she asked, blundering in headfirst.

Curtis looked up from the French fry he had been twiddling between his thumb and his index finger. "Sure," he said, a little defensively, as if he thought it would have been shameful and unmanly to say no.

Elvira pressed on. "You like it?"

"Sure, I like it all right."

"My daddy's a real good fisherman, ain't you, Daddy?"

Hank looked surprised. "Well, I don't know that

I'm so good anymore," he said. "I used to do quite a bit of fishin', but somehow I ain't got around to it much lately."

"Well, I was just thinkin'," Elvira continued. "I was thinkin'—maybe we all ought to go fishin' sometime—what do y'all think about that?"

"Oh, boy, that'd be great!" cried John David, without hesitation. "When can we go? Will you take us, Mr. Trumbull?"

Good old John David, thought Elvira . . .

Hank looked even more surprised. He hemmed and hawed. "Well, er, uh, uh, like I said, I ain't been in a good while . . ."

"Oh, now, John David," put in Miss Ivy, shaking her head, "Mr. Trumbull doesn't have time to take you fishing."

"Sure he does," said Elvira, turning imploring eyes on her father, who looked as if he didn't quite know what to say. "You got time on the weekends, don't you, Daddy? We could all go next Sunday . . ." She tried to emphasize the "all"; it was important that the five of them go—Curtis and Miss Ivy, especially.

"Well, I, uh, I don't know about all of us, Elvira—Miss Ivy prob'ly don't care that much for fishin'." Hank looked over at Miss Ivy—kind of shyly, Elvira judged. He's askin' her for a date, she thought, her heart thumping—that's what he's doin' . . .

"Well, as a matter of fact, Mr. Trumbull," Miss Ivy

said, "I'm not too bad a fisherman myself. Fisher-person, I guess I should say." She smiled. "I used to go with my father when I was a little girl."

"Well, ain't that somethin'," said Hank softly.

He's thinkin' *she's* really somethin', Elvira told herself—he's thinkin' she's smart and pretty and knows how to fish, too . . .

"Mama, can we go then?" cried John David, jumping up and down and tugging impatiently on his mother's arm.

"Oh, I don't know, John David . . ." Miss Ivy looked around helplessly. "Does everybody else really want to go?"

"Yes, ma'am!" cried Elvira—maybe a little too enthusiastically, but she couldn't help it— "We sure do, don't we, Daddy?"

Hank grinned. "Sounds good to me."

Oh, boy, he's a goner, Elvira thought trimphantly.

"What about you, Curtis?" Miss Ivy asked, turning to her older son. "Would you like to go?"

Curtis shrugged. "I don't care."

Aw, c'mon, Curtis—you can do better than that, Elvira thought.

But apparently, that was good enough—

"Well, all right," said Hank. "Sunday morning, then."

It was all Elvira could do to keep from shouting out loud.

They watched Bugs Bunny and the Roadrunner

after supper—just to make sure the television was still working okay. At least, that was Hank's excuse for hanging around, but Elvira felt quite sure that it wasn't the television he cared about so much. She was on top of the world. It seemed to her that Bugs Bunny had never been so clever or Elmer Fudd so funny or the Coyote so wonderfully stupid; she laughed till it hurt.

They lingered a little while on the front steps when it was over. It was a beautiful night—soft and warm and sweet smelling, with the stars shining their hearts out way up high and the katydids singing their summer song down below and the fragrance of Miss Ivy's flowers floating all around—just the right sort of night for falling in love. Not that Hank and Miss Ivy's conversation was very loverlike, but Elvira could read between the lines . . .

"Well," said Hank, "we really ought to get an early start on Sunday—daybreak's the best time to catch fish."

He wants to spend every second of the day with her, Elvira told herself.

"Whatever you think, Mr. Trumbull," said Miss Ivy. "It's so nice of you to take us; the boys are just thrilled."

She means that she's thrilled, thought Elvira—no question about it.

"Well, how 'bout if we pick y'all up about four-thirty, then," suggested Hank, "unless that's too early for you?"

Oh, he's just crazy about her, thought Elvira—that's for durn sure—listen how considerate he's bein'.

"No, no—four-thirty's fine—no sense in going too late and missing the fish," said Miss Ivy.

She respects his judgment, concluded Elvira. And look how her face kinda lights up all over when she talks to him— oh, it's love all right—it's just bound to be love!

15

It was still pitch black when the alarm went off at four o'clock Sunday morning, but Elvira was already awake. She had hardly slept; she was way too excited to sleep. But she felt fine; she liked the feel of the early morning wrapping around her—the dark and the quiet and the secret of it—it felt as if the whole, silent world was waiting for something big to happen . . .

A bird began to sing outside—a clear, two-noted warble. Elvira whistled back. She was full of music this morning; hope was singing in her heart like a crazed canary.

She dressed quickly, but Hank was even quicker. He was already in the kitchen fixing himself some coffee when she walked in.

"You better have some breakfast," he told her. "No tellin' when we'll stop to eat again."

"I ain't hungry." She was too excited to be hungry.

"Well, have a little somethin', anyhow. I don't want you gettin' faintified—we got a long way to go."

"Where are we goin'?" Elvira asked. She hadn't thought to find out before.

"I thought we'd try the jetties over in Galveston—the fishin' used to be real good over there. Acourse, I don't know how it'll be anymore—it's been a long time since I was there."

"I bet it'll be just fine," Elvira said happily. Galveston was perfect. Everything was perfect.

Night bugs were still fluttering drunkenly around the porch light when Hank's pickup truck pulled into Miss Ivy's driveway. Miss Ivy and the boys were waiting outside. John David looked as if he might bust wide open any minute, he was so keyed up.

"I'm gonna catch the biggest fish of all—maybe even a shark!" he shouted, as Hank and Elvira climbed out of the truck.

"Hush up, John David—you're gonna wake the whole neighborhood," said Curtis, but he didn't really look all that mad. I bet he's excited, too, Elvira decided, only he's tryin' not to show it.

"Well, what do you think, Mr. Trumbull?" Miss Ivy smiled at him. "Does this feel to you like the right kind of day for catching fish?"

"You never can tell." Hank grinned. "All we need's a little luck."

We got luck, Elvira told herself. We got plenty of luck . . .

The front of the truck was too small for everybody to scrunch in together, so the children got to ride in back with two big grocery sacks that Miss Ivy had packed with food and an ice chest full of cold drinks and fishing poles and Hank's old tackle box and some nets and a big bucket. John David waved to every car they passed and shouted, "We're goin' fishin'!" to anybody who might happen to be listening. Curtis was mortified.

"Cut that out, John David—everybody's gonna be lookin' at us," he told him.

But Elvira didn't mind people looking; she didn't mind it one bit. I bet they all think we're a family, she thought contentedly. A regular family.

She wished she could hear what Hank and Miss Ivy were saying to each other up in front. She could see them through the back window; they seemed to be getting along just fine. They weren't really talking all that much, but every now and then one of them would say something, and the other one would smile and nod, or maybe laugh. They look real natural together, Elvira assured herself—real natural—they sure do . . .

They had to take the ferry across the bay from Bolivar. The sun was just coming up. There was a rosy glow in the sky that turned the water an iridescent blue-black, with silvery tips. The gulls were awake, filling the air with their cries and swooping down close to the ferry to catch the pieces of potato chips that the children flung to them. The air smelled good—salty and fishy. Elvira leaned out over the edge of the boat and let the spray hit her face as they splashed through the gentle waves.

Galveston was just waking up as the pickup truck rolled off the ferry. They stopped for bait at a place called Will's and got a bucketful of mud minnows; Hank said that minnows were better bait than shrimp, but Elvira suspected that the real reason they were better was that they were cheaper. Then they headed on out past the seawall and over to the south jetty.

The jetty was a long line of huge rocks that had been piled up a hundred years ago on the ocean side of Galveston; it pointed out into the water like an old, gray finger, craggy on the top and full of barnacles on the bottom.

"Now, y'all watch your step," called Hank, starting out onto the rocks. "Sometimes it gets pretty slippery out here." He looked back over his shoulder. Elvira was making her way cautiously, and Miss Ivy had John David by the hand, in spite of his protests, but Curtis was acting pretty cocky; he was leaping along recklessly from rock to rock.

"Whoa, fella! Slow down there," Hank hollered, turning around and walking back. "If you fall in, you'll scare all the fish away."

"I won't fall in," said Curtis. "I'm used to this kind of thing—my dad takes me places like this all the time."

Sure he does, thought Elvira, but she kept her mouth closed.

"Well, maybe," said Hank steadily, "but it won't hurt you none to watch your step, all the same."

Curtis shrugged, but he slowed down. Elvira felt proud of Hank. He had showed who was boss without losing his temper.

They went out pretty far on the rocks, past most of the other fishermen, and found a nice, flat place to put their stuff and get set up. Curtis tried to act like he knew how to bait a hook, but he stuck himself twice and finally had to let his mother help him. Hank was busy getting John David and Elvira squared away.

"Y'all ought to stick to fishin' over here on the calm side," said Hank, when everybody was ready. "The rough side's a little too dangerous. If you fell in over there, you'd have to fight a bad current, and it's deeper, too."

"I've been takin' swimmin' lessons at the Y," said Curtis. "My dad wouldn't mind if I fished on the rough side."

Hank looked as if he was thinking about getting mad, but then he seemed to change his mind. It was his turn to shrug.

"Suit yourself, then . . ."

Miss Ivy looked embarrassed. "Curtis, we're with Mr. Trumbull today, and if he says the rough side is too dangerous, then we'll just stick to the calm side," she said firmly.

"Yes, ma'am," Curtis said. But he didn't look too happy about it.

Oh, come on, Curtis, Elvira wanted to yell at him. *Quit actin' like such a pill—you're gonna spoil everything . . .*

Hank and Miss Ivy spent the next little while showing Elvira and John David how to cast and reel in and cast again. Curtis, naturally, pretended to already know all about how to do it, but Elvira could tell that he was paying attention, too. They all got the hang of it pretty quickly; there were only a few snarled lines, and pretty soon there were five corks—"poppin' corks," Hank called them—bobbing in the gentle water on the calm side of the jetty. The sun was well up now, but it still wasn't as hot as it would be back in Calder by this time; the air was fresher and cooler, blowing off the water. Elvira felt good. Everyone was quiet; there was no sound but the wind and the waves and the cry of the gulls. Elvira watched Hank out of the corner of her eye. She felt quite sure that he kept stealing admiring glances at Miss Ivy, and that it wasn't just her fishing he was admiring . . .

All of a sudden, Curtis let out a yell. "I've got one!" he cried. "My cork went under!"

"Okay—reel it in," said Hank. "Here, Miss Ivy, bring that net over here—easy, now . . ."

Curtis's hook popped out of the water, minus its minnow. His face, which had lit up in excitement, darkened again. "I lost him."

"I bet it was crabs," said Hank. "If it'd been a fish, you'da got him for sure. Do you remember—did your cork go under all at once, or did it kinda bob in and out?"

Curtis looked humiliated, but before he could answer, there was another cry—this time it was John David.

"I think it's a shark!" he yelled. "Look at my fishin' pole!" Sure enough, the pole was bent down, and the reel was spinning wildly.

Hank hurried over to him, put his big hands on top of John David's little ones, and helped him get hold of the reel.

"That's right—you're doin' fine—just keep reelin' . . . all right, now, Miss Ivy, bring that net under him . . . Well, look at that—you got yourself a speck, buddy!"

It was a beautiful fish—whitish on the belly, bluish-gray on top, with a lot of black spots along its sides and tail.

"He's a dandy, John David!" exclaimed Miss Ivy.

"And he was a fighter, too," said Hank. "I don't believe he was too keen on the idea of gettin' caught."

"But I caught him, anyhow," said John David proudly. "And I'm gonna eat him for dinner—can we have him for dinner tonight, Mama?"

"We certainly can—we'll have a celebration—a fish fry—how's that?"

"Way to go, John David," said Curtis. "You got the first fish. But I'm gonna get the next one."

Now he's jealous, worried Elvira. Oh, come on, Curtis—I hope you do get the next fish . . .

But he didn't. For a long time after that, nobody caught anything. The sun got higher and hotter, and Miss Ivy went around putting globs of white sunscreen on everybody's nose. A little later, they took a break and had some of the sandwiches and soft drinks. That perked everybody up quite a bit. And then, for some reason, the fish decided to start biting. Hank caught two good-sized mackerel, and Miss Ivy caught a silly-looking thing that had both its eyes on one side of its head—Hank said it was called a flounder—and Elvira caught something he called a ladyfish—they had to throw it back, because Hank said ladyfish weren't good eating, but Elvira didn't care. She was having a wonderful time—the best time she had ever had in her whole life. If only Curtis would catch a fish and be happy, then everything would be perfect.

But it looked like it just wasn't Curtis's day. There wasn't a fish that would come near his hook, no matter what he did, although the crabs were only too glad to drop by and gnaw on his bait. And his fingers ached, from when he had stuck them, and he was hot and tired and sweaty and sick of the whole thing. It wasn't right, it seemed to him, that some strange man should be taking his family fishing—it ought to be his own daddy who did that. He didn't say it; he didn't have to. Elvira could tell easily enough. Come on, Holy Ghost, she prayed—just one little fish—that ain't any big deal . . .

As if in answer, Curtis's cork disappeared.

"Hey, Curtis—look!" Elvira shouted. "Your cork's gone under!"

Curtis was lying on his back with one arm thrown over his eyes. He sat up listlessly. "Aw, it's prob'ly just crabs again . . ." But even as he said it, his reel started spinning . . .

"You got somethin'!" cried Hank, and everybody

else started yelling, too, and for the next few minutes Curtis was the star of the show . . .

"There you go," Hank encouraged him. "Easy now—you got a tough one—now, don't jerk the line—you don't want to break it—give him a little slack there . . . Good, that's real good—bring him in now . . . You can do it . . . That's it, that's it—here, Miss Ivy, get ready with that net . . . Well, would you look at that!"

It was the biggest, ugliest fish Elvira had ever seen—it had googly eyes and fat lips and wiry whiskers and a wicked-looking fin on its back.

"A catfish!" Miss Ivy laughed exultantly. "A great big catfish, Curtis—that's wonderful!"

"That's a gaff-top—best saltwater catfish there is," said Hank, smiling and taking the net. "You handled that ol' devil just right, son. Nobody coulda done it better."

"Boy, Curtis, he's a nice one, ain't he?" said Elvira happily. "Ain't you glad we came fishin'?"

"Sure, I guess," said Curtis, doing his best to look as if he caught a giant-sized catfish every day of his life. But Elvira wasn't fooled for a minute; she could see that he was just as pleased as he could be. And Hank had called him son . . .

They didn't catch many more fish, so after a while they decided to go on over to the beach and swim.

The water was warm and wonderful. The children hooted and hollered and jumped over the waves and hunted for sand dollars and had a great time. Hank and Miss Ivy sat in the sand and watched; every so often, Elvira would turn and wave to them, and they would smile and wave back . . . The afternoon sun was slanting on them sideways and turning them all golden and glowing . . . They look like one of them romantic cards at the drugstore, thought Elvira—one of them cards with two people holdin' hands on a beach, and the sun goin' down behind the water, and inside it says somethin' real pretty like: REMEMBERING YOU or THE MYSTERY OF LOVE IS EVER NEW WITH YOU.

It wasn't exactly the same . . . The sun wasn't sinking into the sea; it was setting off to the side, behind a restaurant with a giant crab balanced on its roof. And they weren't holding hands. And Elvira couldn't remember any of the people on the cards ever having white globs on their noses. But it was close enough —plenty close enough—she wasn't about to complain . . .

Curtis spent the whole trip home sitting right next to the cooler with the fish in it. He opened it every ten minutes or so to check on his catfish—just to make sure it was really as big as he remembered. John David was sound asleep, with his head pillowed in

Elvira's lap. Miss Ivy and Hank were sitting together quietly in front. The stars had come out. Elvira leaned her head back and gazed contentedly at the sky. *Star light, star bright . . .*

I wish we could just go on and on like this, she thought . . . On and on and on . . . If I could pick a moment—one moment that would last forever—I'd pick this one. This one would do just fine.

It was nine o'clock when they turned into Miss Ivy's driveway. Hank came around to the back of the truck, lifted John David out of Elvira's lap, and carried him into the house. Elvira marveled at how gently he went about it. She wondered if he had ever picked her up and carried her that way, when she was too little or too sleepy to know anything . . .

"Are we still gonna have our fish fry?" asked Curtis, as he and Elvira helped Miss Ivy unload the back of the truck.

"It's a little late for that tonight, don't you think?" answered Miss Ivy. "John David's just worn out—I'll bet both of you are, too."

"Not me—I'm not a bit tired," insisted Curtis.

Miss Ivy smiled and rumpled his hair. "I wish I had half your energy. To tell the truth, I'm the one who's tired. We'll fry your fish tomorrow night—how's that? Mr. Trumbull has offered to clean them for us—isn't that nice of him?"

"Well, all right, I guess I can wait till tomorrow," said Curtis. He looked a little disappointed, but his eyes lit up as another thought struck him. "Is it okay if I go call Daddy and tell him about my fish?"

Elvira imagined she saw the pretty lips fold up a little too tightly for just a second, but then Miss Ivy nodded and said, "I guess it's not too late for that. Go ahead."

Curtis ran off happily into the house just as Hank was coming outside.

"Tell Mr. Trumbull thank-you for the good time!" Miss Ivy called, but Curtis didn't hear.

"Oh, that's all right," said Hank, looking embarrassed.

"It was a wonderful day," said Miss Ivy gratefully, holding out her hand.

Hank took it and turned red as a beet. "It was my pleasure," he mumbled. He looked down shyly into the blue eyes. Elvira held her breath. She had the feeling that he might be about to say something important . . .

"We'd better be goin' on home and gettin' those fish cleaned," said Hank.

Elvira sighed. Not this time, she told herself—but it won't be long now . . .

She rode up in front with Hank on the way back to the trailer park. She felt good. Tired, but happy and so, so hopeful—the hope that had been singing inside her all day long was louder than ever now; she wondered that Hank couldn't hear it, too.

But as the pickup turned into the Happy Trails and pulled up next to the Trumbulls' trailer, the singing stopped abruptly. There was a silver Oldsmobile parked out in front. Its license plate said: TEXAS—DARLA B.

16

Hank muttered something under his breath, but Elvira didn't say anything. She had just turned to stone.

Aunt Darla was sitting on the steps of the trailer. Uncle Roy and Roy Jr. were sitting there, too, but they were unimportant—invisible, almost. It was only Aunt Darla that Elvira really saw. There was no way not to see her. She was even fatter than Elvira remembered. Aunt Darla stood up as Hank turned off the motor of the pickup.

"Surprise, surprise!" she sang out, in that irritating treble that was all too familiar. "We got sick of Padre Island and decided to go home early. We tried to call you—where've you been all day? And where's my little girl?"

I ain't your little girl, thought Elvira. Not in a pig's eye . . . She didn't say it out loud. She couldn't. Stone tongues don't talk.

Hank's face was strained. "Go on, Elvira. Get out and speak to your relatives."

Elvira didn't move. She couldn't. Stone legs don't walk. She looked helplessly at Hank, but his eyes didn't seem to really see her . . . When was it they had looked at her like that before?

"Go on, Elvira," he repeated tonelessly. "Where's your manners?"

Gone, thought Elvira. Dead and gone, dead and gone—ain't nothin' I can do to get 'em back . . .

But Aunt Darla wasn't so easily put off. She heaved herself up, marched majestically around to the other side of the pickup, and opened the door herself.

"Well, there you are, Ellie!" she exclaimed, reaching in and gathering Elvira to her. The girl all but disappeared in a warm, damp, suffocatingly sweet-smelling embrace. Melted popsicles, thought Elvira—she smells like melted popsicles . . . Just don't let her start cryin' on me . . . I couldn't stand that . . .

But the big, old snuffly tears were already rolling down Aunt Darla's cheeks and splashing onto the child's pale hair. Elvira felt them and shuddered. She couldn't help it.

"My, my—look how big you got," sniffled Aunt Darla. "I cain't hardly believe it! Pretty, too—isn't she pretty, Roy?"

Uncle Roy just sort of grunted; he was seldom called upon to actually speak. Aunt Darla generally took care of any speaking that had to be done. She gushed on . . .

"Oh, I can just hardly wait to get you to Sulphur Springs and buy you some nice clothes! Your Aunt Darla's goin' to show you off all over the place—won't we have a good time?"

Great, thought Elvira hopelessly. Just great.

Aunt Darla turned to Hank and spoke to him in a loud whisper over Elvira's head. "My goodness, Hank, where on earth have you taken this child? She smells—fishy!"

"That's because we've been fishin'," said Hank flatly.

"Fishing? Well, if that isn't just like a man—takin' a little girl where *he* wants to go instead of where she wants to go . . . That's exactly the kind of thing I've been talking about, isn't it, Roy? I can see I haven't come a minute too soon." Aunt Darla sniffed scornfully, causing a couple of fat tears to fly off the end of her nose and plop onto Elvira's bare arm. This was too much. Elvira found her voice.

"I-I like f-fishin'," she stammered, gagging a little as she wiped off the wet spots with the back of her hand.

"Well, would you listen to that?" cried Aunt Darla. "Tryin' so hard to please her daddy—it just breaks my heart, that's all . . ." Her voice broke dramatically.

"Well, why don't we all go inside and sit down?" said Hank in that same flat tone, after an embarrassing minute or two of everybody standing around watching Aunt Darla blubber. "Y'all ain't plannin' to drive all the way to Sulphur Springs tonight, are you?"

Aunt Darla was still too overcome to answer; she motioned to Uncle Roy that he should explain.

"No, it's a good six hours from here," he said. "Darla thought that would be too much to try to make tonight. We're stayin' over at the motel till tomorrow mornin'."

Aunt Darla got hold of herself—it was really quite a remarkable recovery—and added, "Of course, we wanted to give our little girl a chance to do her packing—not that she has to worry about taking much . . ." Here she stopped and looked disapprovingly at Elvira's attire . . . "As I was saying before, Ellie, we're going to be getting you a whole new wardrobe once we get to Sulphur Springs . . . Oh, we're going to have such fun! I cain't wait to introduce you to Mary Kay Pickett—she's just your age, and she lives right around the corner from us—she has the sweetest little doll collection . . ."

Aunt Darla kept chattering on as Hank unlocked the trailer door and led the way inside. They all sat down in the cramped living room. Elvira didn't really listen to what Aunt Darla was saying; she suspected that nobody ever really listened to her—it would be such a waste of time . . . She just sat there, thinking stupidly about Mary Kay Pickett's dolls. Elvira hated dolls. She had liked them all right when she was little, but then one time she had seen an old *Night Gallery* rerun about a doll that turned mean and started eating people. She had never trusted dolls after that . . .

Now Aunt Darla was going on about how awful Padre Island had been.

"Not worth a nickel," she declared, and was about to elaborate when Roy Jr. surprised everyone by speaking up—

"I liked it all right," he said quietly.

"Oh, don't be silly," said Aunt Darla. "You only thought you liked it—nobody could really like that awful place, with the water that putrid shade of green—they called it a blossoming of algae, but I didn't see any blossoms—and there was something wrong with the sun, too—you know how it aggravated your acne . . ."

At this, Roy Jr. turned a brilliant shade of scarlet and said no more. Elvira might have felt sorry for him if she could have felt anything at all.

"But the sand was the worst," Aunt Darla went on, shaking her head. "I just cain't stand sand—it gets into everything in those beach houses—I don't know how people tolerate it. I suppose they're just not as keen on housekeeping as I am. I tell you, that sand just makes my flesh crawl."

"That's the thing about islands," said Hank dully. "It's so hard to find one that don't have sand."

That's a jokc, thought Elvira just as dully. He's makin' a joke . . .

But Aunt Darla appeared not to have heard. She talked on a little longer, and then she said that they really ought to be going, since they'd want to get an early start in the morning. "We'll be by for you at eight, Ellie—eight on the nose—I pride myself on being punctual, don't I, Roy?"

"That she does," nodded Uncle Roy—a little grimly, it seemed to Elvira.

"Now, you get a good night's rest," Aunt Darla said, giving the girl one more paralyzing squeeze. "Tomorrow you'll be starting on a whole new life." Her eyes moistened up again. "I just imagine your sweet mother in heaven is crying tears of joy at this very minute," she sniveled.

I don't want a whole new life, thought Elvira. My old one's all right . . . And I bet my mama ain't no crybaby . . .

When they had gone, Hank and Elvira sat in zombielike silence in the living room. It was as if there had been another death in the family.

We were so close, thought Elvira. Everything was goin' so good—and then Aunt Darla had to go and spoil it all by comin' early . . .

"Well," said Hank finally, because somebody had to say something. "Well, I guess you ought to be gettin' to bed."

"Yessir."

"You got a big day ahead of you tomorrow."

"I guess so."

Hank was thirsty. He had never been so thirsty. He stood up and walked over to the kitchen. He opened the icebox. It was empty. He slammed it shut.

"Look, I got to go out for a while. You go on to bed. I'll see you in the mornin', before you—well, I'll see you then."

"Yessir."

He left. Elvira stood up slowly, walked exactly ten steps back to her sleeping nook, and lay down on the bed. She didn't go to the bathroom or brush her teeth or bathe—she really needed to bathe—she was all sticky from the beach water. And she *was* filthy—Aunt Darla had said she smelled fishy, and she had been right. But it didn't matter. She might never bathe again. What did it matter? Maybe if she got dirty enough, Aunt Darla would send her back—she had said she couldn't stand dirt . . . No, it was sand—she couldn't stand sand, that was it—Aunt Darla hated sand . . . Well, maybe the sand hates you, too, Aunt Darla—just like I do—didja ever think of that? I bet you never thought of that . . .

She drifted into a troubled sleep and dreamed a succession of senseless dreams . . . She was standing on an old sunken hulk out in Galveston Bay, watching Hank try to fix spaghetti over an open fire, but he didn't do it right—he was pouring the raw noodles into the sauce . . . You don't do it like that, she tried to yell at him—you got to read the label . . . But he couldn't hear her or see her, either—she was invisible—she was a ghost . . . She was kneeling in Miss Ivy's garden, pulling weeds, only instead of a weed she pulled up Curtis's catfish—"Throw me back," it told her—"There ain't gonna be no fish fry—you forgot to clean me . . ." She was standing on the jetty, but she got too close to the rough side, and she fell in—but it wasn't water at all—it was a toy store filled with dolls—Aunt Darla dolls that whined and tried to bite her . . .

Thunder rumbled darkly in the distance, and Elvira

opened her eyes. The smell of rain drifted in through the window screen . . .

All of a sudden she was wide awake. The stony feeling was gone. Her heart was beating fast, and her breath was coming fast—just like it had done that other time—that time when . . . when whatever it was had come to her—she had thought it was the Holy Ghost, but she didn't know what she should call it now . . . It didn't matter, anyway. She knew what she had to do.

She got up and looked in Hank's bedroom. He wasn't there. She walked into the kitchen and checked the clock. It was 11:48. Thank the Lord there was time. Eight o'clock in the morning was still a long way off.

She opened the trailer and looked around. There was nobody in sight. That was good; she didn't want to have to think up excuses for being out in the middle of the night. She started running—silently—her bare feet making almost no noise as she flew along in the darkness. There were pools of murky yellow where the street lamps cast their sickly light, but she avoided those. She was no more than a shadow, a breath of wind, a piece of the night . . .

It thundered again. It would rain before long. That would do her garden good; it had been too long since the last rain—the rice farmers were all bellyaching . . .

She had never run so fast. She made it to South

Street in less than fifteen minutes—a new world's record, she told herself, as she stood, panting, on Miss Ivy's doorstep. It was way too late to go visiting, but that didn't matter. This was an emergency. She rang the doorbell. She waited a minute, then she rang it again, longer and harder. Now she could hear movement in the house and see lights being turned on. Then the curtain of the window by the front door was parted, and Miss Ivy's face peered out. She gasped when she saw Elvira.

"Elvira, sweetheart—what on earth—what's wrong?" she exclaimed, as she opened the door.

"I'm sorry to come so late, Miss Ivy, but I got to talk to you." The words tumbled on top of each other. Elvira could barely get it all out—she was still breathing hard.

"Well, of course—come right in, darlin'—calm down, now—that's right—you just tell Miss Ivy all about it." She sounded so sweet and kind and concerned, as she put her arm around Elvira's shoulders and led her gently away from the door and over to the couch, that it was all the girl could do to keep herself from dissolving into a disgusting puddle of tears. But, somehow, she managed; this was no time to break down and be stupid—she had to keep a clear head.

"It's—it's about my daddy," she began, and then she stopped—she wanted to put it just right . . .

"What's happened to him, Elvira? Has there been an accident? Is he sick?"

Elvira shook her head. "No, ma'am—he's all right—we're both all right. He's—he's asleep; he don't know I'm here . . ." She stopped again, flustered by her half-truth.

Miss Ivy waited for her to continue.

Elvira took a deep breath and went on. "Miss Ivy—you like my daddy, don't you?"

The angel-lady looked surprised. "Of course I do, Elvira. He's a very nice man."

"Yes, ma'am, but, well—do you think you might like him more than—more than just a little bit?" Somehow, Elvira couldn't bring herself to say the word "love" . . .

"I'm not sure I know exactly what you mean, Elvira." Miss Ivy spoke slowly—ever so slowly and gently.

There ain't no sense in beatin' around the bush, Elvira told herself. Just spit it out, girl—spit it out—your life's on the line here . . .

She took another deep breath. "I mean, well, do you think you might like him enough to marry him?" She looked into her lap as she said it; somehow, she couldn't bear to look into the blue eyes right now. For a moment, no one said anything. There was a soft, rushing sound from outside; the rain had begun.

When Miss Ivy spoke again, it was in that same slow, gentle voice. "I've only known your father a short time, sweetheart. Not nearly long enough to be thinking about him in that way. And I'm sure he feels the same about me . . ."

"Oh, no, ma'am," said Elvira earnestly. She looked up now, and her heart and soul were in her eyes. "He'd be glad to marry you, if you wanted him to. I just know it—it's writ all over him. Why, anybody'd love you, Miss Ivy." There. She had said it.

But Miss Ivy only shook her head. "Elvira, I can't possibly marry your father. I don't plan on marrying anyone for a long, long time—maybe never. So you mustn't think about it anymore." Her voice was still gentle, but it was firm, too.

Elvira's heart sank. She sat very still. She stared at her fingernails; they were filthy, she noted absently. "Then you don't really like him," she said quietly. "Why'd you act like you liked him, if you didn't?"

"But I do—I like him very much," said Miss Ivy. "He's been so kind to the boys and me this last week—and even if he hadn't been, I'd still like him, just because he's your father. Why, I believe I'd like anyone who was related to you." She lifted Elvira's chin, but Elvira shook her head free and looked down into her lap again.

"No, ma'am, you wouldn't—you wouldn't like Aunt Darla, and she's kin to me," said Elvira hopelessly.

"Aunt Darla? You never told me anything about your Aunt Darla."

Elvira sighed. "There ain't much to tell. She's a big old fat lady who lives in Sulphur Springs. She's got a whole lot of money. If you don't marry my daddy, I gotta go live with her."

Miss Ivy's mouth dropped open. "You what?"

"I gotta go live at her house. She thinks she knows more about raisin' girls than my daddy does, and he's worried about not havin' a steady job and all . . ."

Miss Ivy looked thoughtful. "I see . . . and you don't want to go live with her?"

Fire came back into Elvira's soul. "No, ma'am," she said. "I don't want to go near her, if I can help it."

"Why don't you like her, Elvira?"

"Because . . ." Elvira floundered for a reason that wouldn't sound too stupid. " 'Cause one time she said my dress was tacky, and she calls me Ellie, and she's always cryin' and slobberin' all over me, and—and—she's *fat,*" she finished up desperately. "Oh, Miss Ivy, couldn't you marry Hank? It'd be so good for everybody—your boys like him, and they need a daddy . . ."

Miss Ivy looked startled. "They already have a daddy, Elvira."

"Aw, but he ain't no good, Miss Ivy—playin' sick and lettin' 'em down about Astroworld and all, and he musta been mean to you or you never woulda left him."

"No, Elvira, you're mistaken—he's a fine man and

a good father. He really was sick when he didn't take the boys to Astroworld . . . And if he and I didn't get along—well, that was just as much my fault as it was his—probably more mine."

Elvira couldn't stand to hear Miss Ivy criticized, even by Miss Ivy herself. "That cain't be true, Miss Ivy—you're so sweet and good to everybody!" she cried. "You're—you're like an angel!"

Miss Ivy sighed and smoothed Elvira's frazzled forehead. "I'm no angel, sweetheart—not by a long shot. I wish I were really as good as you think I am, but it's not as simple as that . . . I don't believe there are any angels—or devils, either—not here on this earth, anyway. Just people—people who are good some of the time and bad some of the time, every one of us. Why, I'll bet even your Aunt Darla isn't nearly as awful as you think she is right now. She must love you a lot if she wants you to live with her . . ."

Yes, she is awful, thought Elvira. She's every bit as awful as I think she is . . .

She didn't say it out loud. It was no use arguing. She had said everything there was to say, and Miss Ivy still wasn't about to marry Hank. She didn't love him one bit; it had all been a mistake. Well, then, if that was the way it was, all right; Elvira wasn't going to shame herself by begging any more than she already had. She still had some pride left. She sat there for a moment, steeling herself against the soothing sensation of Miss Ivy's hand stroking her hair. Then she stood up.

"I'm sorry I bothered you. I got to go home now."

Miss Ivy stood up, too. "It's so late, Elvira—why don't you stay here the rest of the night? We can call your father and tell him where you are."

Elvira shook her head. "No, ma'am, we cain't. They ain't nobody who answers the pay phone this time of night. I'll just run on home."

"No, you won't, either," Miss Ivy said firmly. "It's the middle of the night, and it's raining cats and dogs out there. If you really have to go, I'll drive you. The boys will be all right by themselves for ten minutes. Just wait a second while I throw on some clothes and tell Curtis what I'm doing . . ."

"Yes, ma'am," said Elvira. It really didn't matter. Nothing mattered.

The rain was coming down in sheets now. Elvira and Miss Ivy were silent on the drive over to the trailer park; the night had too many voices already—the downpour and the deafening thunder and the steady *swish, swish* of the windshield wipers . . .

The pickup truck was still parked right beside the trailer; Hank had walked to wherever it was he had gone. Elvira was glad of that. She didn't want Miss Ivy to know that she had lied about Hank's being home asleep. It was just too hard to explain; she was sick of talking.

"Thanks for the ride," she murmured, when the car came to a stop. She started to open the door, but Miss Ivy leaned over and caught her hand.

"Elvira," she said. She practically had to shout to make herself heard over the storm.

"Yes, ma'am," said Elvira, without turning around. She didn't think she could stand to look at Miss Ivy's face any more tonight. It hurt too much.

"Elvira, I just want you to know that I'm sorry— I'm so sorry I can't do what you want me to do—be who you want me to be . . ."

"That's all right." It wasn't all right; it wasn't anything like all right. But what else could she say? She wished Miss Ivy would just shut up.

"But I'll always be your friend—you know that, don't you?"

"Yes, ma'am." Elvira bit her lip hard, to keep it from trembling. "I-I gotta go now." She grabbed her hand away, threw the door open, and ran—through the rain, up the steps, and into the trailer. She slammed the door with all her strength. That felt good; if she let herself get mad, the throbbing, aching feeling in her throat might go away . . . She waited for Miss Ivy to drive away. Then she opened the door and slammed it again . . . and again . . . and again . . . and every time she slammed it, she shouted, "I hate you! I hate you! I hate you!" She didn't know who it was she hated the most—Miss Ivy or Aunt Darla or Hank or the

Holy Ghost; somehow, they had all become one and the same. She yelled until she was hoarse, but the storm swallowed her cries, and no one heard.

It was well after two in the morning when Hank made his way home. The rain was still coming down hard; he was wet to the skin. He didn't care—it didn't matter—nothing mattered. He reached the trailer. Suddenly, he was struck with the hazy notion that something was amiss—different . . .

It ain't nothin', he told himself—just the rain and the dark . . . Everything looks different in the dark . . .

And then his foot slipped, and he stumbled right into a gaping, slushy hole in the middle of Elvira's garden. The rosebush was gone.

17

For the second time that night, Miss Ivy's doorbell rang. This time it was a series of sharp, staccato rings that set her heart racing and sent her running for the door . . .

Hank Trumbull was standing grimly on the front porch, oblivious to the water that was streaming from nearly every inch of him. His eyes were bloodshot, but otherwise, he appeared to be stone-cold sober.

"Where's my girl? She's here, ain't she?" His voice was hard with an anger born of fear.

Miss Ivy gave a little gasp. "Elvira? She's not at home?"

For a fraction of a second, Hank stared at her uncomprehendingly. Then he pushed past her into the house.

"Elvira!" he shouted, and the whole house shook with the sound of it. "Elvira, you come here this minute—Elvira!" He began stamping through the house. Miss Ivy ran after him, pulling on his wet sleeve and trying to get him to listen to her—

"She's not here, Mr. Trumbull. She was here earlier, but I took her home—I watched her go in the trailer door—I'm telling you, she's not here!"

Hank wheeled around to face her at the foot of the stairs. The fear was plain in his face now. "She's gotta be here—where else would she be?" He turned back around and ran up the stairs, calling his child's name, over and over . . .

Curtis and John David were awakened by the yelling; they stumbled sleepily out of their room and down the stairs to their mother.

"What's wrong, Mama? What's the matter with Mr. Trumbull?" asked Curtis.

Miss Ivy drew both boys close to her. "He can't find Elvira, baby; he's trying to find her . . ."

"She got lost?" John David asked, his eyes wide.

"I—I don't know—I'm afraid so . . . but it's going to be all right—he'll find her—I'll help him find her . . . You boys go back to bed—I'll call Mrs. McFaddin to come stay with you in case I have to go out . . ."

"I could help you, Mama," said Curtis. "Let me help find her."

"Me, too, Mama—I can help!" cried John David.

"No, you can help the most by going back to bed like big boys. You'll do that for Mama, won't you—and for Elvira?" Her voice trembled a little.

John David started to cry, but Curtis took his hand and pulled him back up the stairs. "It's okay—I'll take care of him. Y'all go find Elvira . . ."

"You don't hafta pull on me—I can walk by my own self!" wailed John David . . .

Hank passed the boys on his way down. Something in his eyes made them afraid of him, and they turned and ran.

His face was ashen. "She ain't up there," he mumbled stupidly, as he started for the front door.

Miss Ivy followed. "Wait, Mr. Trumbull—you'll need to use my phone—don't you think you'd better call the police?"

Hank stopped and ran his fingers wildly through his hair. "Yeah," he murmured. "Yeah, I guess I better . . ."

Miss Ivy led him into the kitchen and handed him the phone. He picked up the receiver and dialed the emergency number that was printed on the inside . . .

"This is Henry S. Trumbull," he said hoarsely. "You gotta help me—my little girl's gone."

She hadn't taken anything with her but the rosebush. She had to take that. She was sorry to leave the other plants—the fall flowers—but she figured they had had a good start; they might be all right without her. It was only the rosebush that really needed her.

She knew it was stupid to run away, just like all those dumb kids in all those dumb movies, but she couldn't help it. It had come to her, somewhere around the fortieth time she slammed the trailer door, that it was the only thing she could do—there was nothing else left. She hadn't had time to think out a good plan; she had just dug up the rosebush, stuck it in a brown grocery sack—DOUBLE STRENGTH—NO NEED FOR DOUBLE-BAGGING—and walked away through the pouring rain.

The rain was good, in a way. It beat down so hard on her head that she couldn't think—she could only keep putting one foot in front of the other, like a machine—right, then left, then right again. She just kept walking and walking and walking, and the rain kept raining and raining and raining . . .

She crossed the highway when no cars were in sight

and then walked along parallel to it—but far enough back so she couldn't be seen. It would have been easier walking on the shoulder of the road, but somebody would have been sure to notice her and stop and ask what a kid was doing walking along the highway in the middle of the night. So she stuck to the ditches and fields, sloshing along in mud and muck up to her ankles—her knees, it felt like sometimes. She wouldn't let herself think further ahead than the next minute—the next step, even. She knew that Houston was somewhere up ahead—a place so big that it could swallow up anybody—even Aunt Darla; one skinny little kid shouldn't have any trouble being invisible there. But the idea of Houston was vague, unreal . . . Nothing was real but the night and the rain and her two tired feet.

Right, then left, then right again . . .

The police acted quickly, but not quickly enough to suit Hank. "Why don't they come? What's takin' 'em so long?" he asked over and over, as he paced frantically from one end of the house to the other.

"It's only been ten minutes, Mr. Trumbull," Miss Ivy tried to reassure him. "I'm sure they'll be right over . . ."

But when the police car pulled into the driveway minutes later, Hank was still far from feeling reassured; only one young man got out of it—a young punk, Hank judged, as soon as he saw him. "Officer Greene," he said his name was—a redheaded, serious-eyed fellow with a deliberate way of going about his business that nearly drove Hank right off the deep end. It seemed to him that Officer Greene took forever asking questions and writing down answers. Even something as simple as a description of Elvira took a lot longer than it should have—

"She's just a little bit of a thing," Hank told him. "I don't know how tall, exactly—somethin' under five foot . . ."

"She's about four-eight or nine," put in Miss Ivy.

"I see," said Officer Greene, making a careful note of the information. "Hair color?"

"Kinda—kinda yellowish," stammered Hank . . .

"Light blonde," said Miss Ivy.

"Eyes?"

"Oh, I don't know," said Hank. "They're sort of a funny color—like her mother's . . ."

Officer Greene looked at Miss Ivy. "I'd call that blue," he said.

"I'm not her mother," explained Miss Ivy quietly. She sounded apologetic. "Just a friend. Her eyes are gray—gray-green, sometimes . . ."

The policeman looked from Miss Ivy to Hank. "Excuse me, but this is your house, isn't it?"

Hank looked at him as if he were a complete idiot.

He didn't have time to be standing around here talking to a little boy who was playing cops and robbers—he ought to be out looking for his child . . . "My house? Naw, this ain't my house—I just come here on account of I thought she might be here . . . I told them that on the phone already—don't y'all ever listen to what people are tellin' you?"

Officer Greene stayed calm—way too calm, in Hank's opinion. "I'm sorry, sir; apparently there's been some mix-up. Where is your residence?"

"I live over at the Happy Trails Trailer Park—just off Interstate Ten . . ."

"Is that the last place the child was seen?" asked Officer Greene.

"Well, sure—that's where she lives," Hank said.

"Then we really ought to be starting from there," Officer Greene continued . . .

"All right, then, let's go—what are we waitin' for? I'll lead the way in my pickup . . ." Hank was already out the door and gone before he had finished speaking, leaving Miss Ivy and Officer Greene to follow as best they could . . .

Right foot, then left, then right again . . . Rain and rain and rain some more . . . It's raining, it's pouring, the old man is snoring . . .

Elvira's brain was getting soggy. The rain was washing the sense clean out of her skull. It was just like in those old World War II movies when the bad guys made the good guys go crazy by dripping water on their heads, one drop at a time. Elvira figured that at the rate of a thousand drops per second, she ought to be ready for the loony bin in nothing flat . . . Right foot, then left, then right again . . .

She tripped over a rock and took a nasty tumble. The rosebush scratched her face as she fell. It hurt, but she was too tired to care. Anyway, she figured it was only fair for the rosebush to hurt her, after what she had done to it—digging it up again, just when it was starting to get better.

"But I couldn't help it," she told her plant as she got to her feet. "I couldn't just leave you there—ain't nobody else gonna look out for you—nobody, you hear me?"

It was still dark. She had been walking forever and ever, but it was still dark. The sun ought to be up by now, surely . . . Elvira looked behind her—east was behind her—to see if there was any change in the sky. If there was, she couldn't see it. Well. She had wished for one moment that would last forever, and it looked like she had gotten her wish—only it was the wrong moment—wrong, all wrong . . . Maybe she ought to wish again . . . *Star light, star bright* . . . But there were no stars in the sky now.

Hank paced restlessly back and forth through the trailer, while Officer Greene sat in the living room and took more of his everlasting notes. Miss Ivy had come along to help in any way she could; she was standing in the corner, with her arms folded tightly over her chest.

"Was your little girl upset about anything the last time you saw her?" asked the policeman.

"Well, she musta been—ain't that pretty plain? She didn't really show it, though—she ain't that type."

"Had anything happened that might have upset her?"

"My sister came into town last night. Elvira was s'posed to go with her to Sulphur Springs in the morning—I guess she didn't want to go . . . I don't know—I thought she had changed her mind about it . . ."

"I believe I was the last person to see her," said Miss Ivy in a pained voice. "She was—terribly upset about going to her aunt's . . . She came to me for help, and I—well, I couldn't help her. I'm afraid I only made things worse." She bit her lip, but went on. "I should have known—I should have made her stay at my house and talk about it some more, but she just—closed up all of a sudden and said she had to go home. So I took her back here and watched her go inside . . . I knew she was taking it hard, but I really thought she was going to be all right . . . She's such a strong little thing . . ." Miss Ivy's voice broke.

Officer Greene turned back to Hank. "Have you checked with all her friends? It's possible that she's with one of them."

"She don't have no friends—'cept for this lady and her kids. We—we ain't lived here all that long."

"Well, she may have friends you don't know about," said Officer Greene. "I think we'd better start by knocking on some doors. It's entirely possible that she never left the trailer park."

"I'm tellin' you, she don't have no friends in this place—you're just gonna be wastin' your time . . ."

"Mr. Trumbull, I realize that you're upset, but I have to go about this the best way I know how, and checking with your neighbors is the logical first step. Most children who run away really don't run too far."

"Elvira ain't like most children," said Hank bitterly. "She ain't like anybody but herself. You cain't go lookin' for her in places other children would go . . . Would you stop scribblin' in that book and listen to what I'm tellin' you?"

"I'm just trying to do my job, Mr. Trumbull." Officer Greene's voice was still maddeningly calm . . .

"Excuse me," interrupted Miss Ivy. Her face was taut. "I just found this—I think you'd better look at it." She handed Elvira's spiral notebook to the policeman. It was opened to the list: THINGS I MIGHT DO.

Officer Greene took the notebook and scanned the page. His eyes stopped toward the middle and stayed there for some time. It was more than Hank could stand—

"What's it say? Why are you lookin' at it like that?" He grabbed the notebook away from the policeman.

Officer Greene coughed. "I don't want to alarm you, Mr. Trumbull, but has your daughter ever tried to—harm herself in any way?"

Hank looked up sharply. "What do you mean—harm herself? She wouldn't—I mean, she ain't the type that would . . ." He couldn't bring himself to finish.

Wordlessly Officer Greene pointed to number two. *Tell Hank that I will die if he makes me go. Good side—This is the truth. Bad side—He probly would not beleave me.*

Hank stared uncomprehendingly at the line. Then his mind cleared enough for its meaning to sink in . . . He tried to swallow, but he couldn't; his mouth had gone dry. He shook his head—slowly at first, then more vehemently— "She didn't really mean that—she ain't that type . . . I'm tellin' you, she ain't that type at all!" He was shouting now.

Miss Ivy put her hands to her face. Her shoulders were shaking.

"What are you cryin' for?" yelled Hank. "Ain't nothin' to cry about—Elvira's all right, do you hear me? She's all right . . ."

"Mr. Trumbull," said Officer Greene—there was sympathy in his voice now—"I still think our first step is to check with your neighbors; I'll get started right away."

Hank looked at him in disgust. "Go ahead—waste your time lookin' where she ain't and thinkin' up things she never done—I don't care what you do—you can go straight to the devil for all I care—I'm gonna go find my kid." He threw open the door, got into his pickup, and started driving blindly through the dark, wet night, stopping every block or so to call his daughter's name. "Elvira! Elvira! You come home, do you hear me? Elvira!"

There was no answer but the sound of the falling rain.

Rain, rain, go away, come again some other day . . . Oh, Lord, rain, ain't you never gonna go away?

Right foot, then left, then right again . . . Joshua fit the battle of Jericho and the rain came a-tumblin' down . . . No, those were walls, not rain . . . Right foot, then left, then . . .

Suddenly Elvira stopped. She had come to a river. Without realizing it, she had been climbing gradually upward for the last five minutes or so, and now she found herself standing on the edge of a small cliff. Black water was moving silently beneath her—at least, it seemed silent to her; her ears had long ago become dead to everything but the ceaseless sound of the rain. She looked over at the highway; from where she stood, she could just barely make out the sign in front of the bridge. LOST AND OLD RIVER, it said. Oh, sure, she remembered it now; she had driven this highway with Hank plenty of times. If you were coming from the other direction, from Houston, the sign said OLD AND LOST—not LOST AND OLD. She and Hank had puzzled over that and finally figured out that it wasn't one river, but two that came together right here—the Lost River and the Old River—or the Old River and the Lost River—it didn't matter—it was downright depressing either way . . .

The problem now was—how in the world could she get across it—or them? She didn't see any bridge but the highway bridge, and only a fool would try to walk over that—even in broad daylight, let alone on a night like this; there was no room for a person to walk, none at all. She had to think of some other way . . . But she couldn't think—her brain was total mush now . . . chocolate pudding . . . What's your name? Puddin' and tame—ask me again and I'll tell you the same . . . Oh, Lordy, where'd that come from? She was crazy, for sure . . . And now that her feet had stopped walking, they didn't want to start again; they refused to walk another step. She had to rest, that was all there was to it. She had to close her eyes for just a minute or two, and then she would feel better and be able to think of a way across the water.

She dragged herself a little way more to the north, to where an old, gnarled live oak tree spread its branches over a bit of sandy bank. The tree would keep some of the rain off. Elvira vaguely remembered someone telling her to stay away from trees during thunderstorms, but she was too bone-tired to worry about being struck by lightning. Most of the thunder had stopped, anyway—it was only a far-off growling now. Maybe the rain was going away, after all . . .

Hank drove the night long, looking for Elvira. He drove all over Calder first, stopping and shouting her name over and over again. A few people came out of their houses and shook their fists at him, but he hardly noticed.

He went to the highway after that and drove west toward Houston, trying with all his might to believe that he would come upon her any minute, walking alongside the road. But he never did, he never did . . .

He was halfway across the Lost and Old River before he realized that Elvira couldn't have crossed this bridge; there was no room to walk. If she had come this way at all, she must have stopped when she got to the river. Stopped and—and then, what? He tried to think the way she would think.

And then it came to him again—that line in her notebook—*Tell Hank that I will die if he makes me go. Good side—This is the truth* . . . This is the truth . . . This is the truth . . . The words played over and over in Hank's mind like some horrible, broken record. She didn't mean it, he told himself angrily. She didn't mean it . . . But all the same, as soon as he had crossed the bridge, he turned around, came back across, and pulled off the highway. Then he climbed out of the pickup and half walked, half stumbled along the river bank, calling Elvira's name . . .

Suddenly he saw something up ahead—he couldn't quite make it out—something lying in the water at the river's edge . . . Hank's heart stopped beating. For a moment, he couldn't move. And then he was running, running, running like a madman . . .

It was only a rock. A rock with a kind of yellowish river weed growing on it. It wasn't Elvira—she wasn't lying there, cold and dead, in the shallow water of the Old and Lost River . . .

Relief poured over Hank in a strong, sweet flood. He sank to his knees right there in the water. He wasn't a praying man, but he prayed now. He prayed to God to let him find his little girl . . . He prayed to his dead wife . . . He prayed to anyone who might be listening . . .

I know I ain't been worth a lick as a father, Margaret, but I'll do better . . . Just let her be all right . . . Please, God, please—just let her be all right . . .

He was shaking. For a long time, he knelt there, with his face buried in his hands. He felt so helpless—so old and lost and helpless . . . But gradually, a kind of desperate calm filled him. He pulled himself together, walked back to the pickup, and started driving east. Maybe she had gone east . . .

A faint streak of red appeared on the horizon. The rain had stopped. The night was nearly over.

18

A crawfish wriggled his ugly self out of a burrow and paraded tail-first along the riverbank. It was feeding time. The sun was just up, and the birds were singing. The storm had washed the air clean; a fresh little breeze was ruffling the river water. It was going to be a fine day. The crawfish headed for his usual hunting ground under the old live oak tree; the fattest slugs were always lying around in its shade, ripe for the picking. But when he got there, he stopped in confusion. There was something piled up in his favorite spot. He poked a cautious claw at it. All of a sudden, the something opened its eyes—it had eyes—sat up, and made a terrifying noise. Alarmed, the crawfish skittered away as fast as his spindly little legs could carry him and disappeared down his burrow.

Elvira shuddered. She hadn't meant to scream. She had never been a screamer, but then, she had never before opened her eyes and been nose to nose with a crawfish.

She looked around her. So. The night and the rain had actually ended. Well. That was something, anyway. Her head hurt, and her throat was sore, and she ached all over, but at least it wasn't dark and raining. She couldn't have stood another second of that. And at least she wasn't on her way to Sulphur Springs; that was something, wasn't it? The main thing.

She wondered what time it was. It seemed only minutes ago that she had closed her eyes. For once, she had slept without dreaming. She was all dreamed out.

Her stomach growled. How long had it been since she had eaten—days, weeks, months? No, of course not—they had finished the last of Miss Ivy's sandwiches in the pickup truck on the way back from Galveston—that was only last night. You're all right, she told herself. You ain't gonna die of starvation yet.

There wasn't much traffic on the highway. Elvira looked over at the bridge to see if it might be possible to cross it now. No way—not unless she could flatten herself up against the concrete wall in the middle and inch along like some kind of human snail. No, the bridge was no good. Noah Goode, she thought listlessly. Ha, ha.

She decided to walk around a little and see if there might be any other way across. But when she tried to stand up, she felt so dizzy that she had to sit right back down again. Oh, shoot, she thought—I cain't be sick—this ain't the time to get sick . . .

She leaned her head against the treetrunk, closed her eyes, and watched the crazy speckles of light careening around on the insides of her eyelids. She couldn't remember the last time she had felt this awful; it was a lot worse, even, than that day a thousand years ago when she'd been getting ready to go over to Miss Ivy's for tea . . . Hank had fixed her tomato soup that day. The thought of it brought an unexpected lump to her throat. She pushed it away angrily. She didn't have time to be thinking about tomato soup; she ought to be thinking about what she'd do once she got to Houston. She'd have to make up a story that she could tell people—sooner or later, she was going to have to tell somebody something . . . But her head ached so . . . Shoot, she didn't really feel like thinking—not right now. She could always think later . . . Or maybe she'd just give it up for good; nine times out of ten, it wasn't really worth the trouble, anyway.

A big black ant crawled over her foot and bit her on the toe. Great, just great, she thought. Ants. Black ants that bite. Whoever heard of black ants bitin'? Ain't nothin' the way it's s'posed to be . . . No guarantees worth piddly squat . . .

Her head was really throbbing now. She lay down and closed her eyes again to ease it a little. Maybe if I just rest my eyes for a few more minutes, I'll get to feelin' better, she told herself. Just a few more minutes, and then I'll get goin' and find a way across the river . . .

The next thing she knew, somebody was shaking her shoulder . . . For a second, she thought it was Aunt Darla, come to get her, but when she opened her eyes, all she saw was a little black kid—a girl, maybe about John David's age.

"You all right?" the little girl asked her, cocking her head to one side and looking at her curiously.

Elvira pulled herself up to a sitting position and tried to look casual. "Sure, I'm all right," she lied.

"You crawfishin', too?" asked the girl.

Elvira looked at her blankly. "Crawfishin'?"

"You know, catchin' crawfish—this is where we always come to go crawfishin'. You're in our secret spot."

"Oh. I-I'm sorry," faltered Elvira, getting shakily to her feet. She had to lean on the live oak for support; the world was jiggling around a lot. "I'll go on, then . . . I don't want to be in your way . . ."

"Aw, that's okay—you got here first. What'd you do—sleep here all night? It's real early."

Elvira couldn't think of an answer right off the bat, but the little girl didn't notice, because just then her father and two big brothers showed up.

"Look, y'all—there's somebody in our spot. It ain't a secret spot no more."

The girl's father smiled at Elvira. "Well, aren't you the early bird?" He seemed friendly enough, but something told Elvira that she was in trouble; she ought to be getting away from here as fast as she could. She ought to run. Only she didn't really feel much like running . . . anyhow, that might look suspicious.

"You live around here?" the man went on.

Elvira nodded vaguely.

"Well, you don't mind if we join you, do you? Plenty of crawfish—ought to be enough for all of us."

"No—no, sir," said Elvira weakly, sliding back down along the treetrunk until she was sitting again. She figured that the best thing to do was to try to act normal. Then maybe they'd hurry up and do their crawfishing and go away.

But the strangers didn't seem to be in any hurry. They took their sweet time about every little thing—

looking for sticks and tying bacon on string and tying the string to the sticks and wading out in the water to check their bait and scooping up crawfish with raggedy old nets and laughing and squealing like they didn't have good sense . . . Elvira hated them for being so happy; nobody had any business being that happy . . . She closed her eyes to shut out the sight of all that foolish happiness . . .

A little while later, she heard voices talking nearby, but she couldn't seem to open her eyes. It felt as if her eyelids were glued shut—even when it gradually dawned on her that the voices were talking about her.

"I don't know—I don't think we should just leave her here. Somethin' tells me she's in trouble—maybe a runaway . . ."

"You think there's somethin' wrong with her, Daddy?"

"I'm not sure, honey—maybe she's just tired."

"She looks kinda sick."

"She does, doesn't she? I wonder if she's got a fever . . ."

Elvira felt a cool hand touch her forehead; that was enough to force her eyes open. She sat up. Funny, she couldn't remember lying down . . . There was sand in her mouth.

"I'm all right," she muttered.

"No, you're not; you're hot as a firecracker, missy. Now, why don't you tell us where you live, and we'll take you over there. I bet your mama's worryin' about you right now."

"No, she ain't," said Elvira. This, at least, was no lie—that is, as far as she knew.

"Well, I'm not leaving here without you; I can't have that on my conscience, so you might just as well tell me where you live."

Elvira thought for a minute. It hurt to think, but she had to. This was her chance. She could say that she lived in Houston, and then these people would take her there . . . but where would she go when she got to Houston? This man wouldn't just drop her off somewhere without being sure that somebody was going to watch out for her—she could see it in his eyes. She had known he was dangerous the first second she saw him . . . why hadn't she gotten away then, before it was too late? She had a feeling it was too late now . . .

"Come on, now—we don't mean you any harm, little girl. You just tell us where you live, why don't you?" His voice was so kind. Unnervingly kind. Disastrously kind. It did her in. Elvira opened her mouth to tell another lie, but all that would come out was the truth.

"I live in Calder," she sighed. "For now, anyway."

19

It was Aunt Darla who opened the trailer door when Mr. Lofton—that was his name—knocked on it. So she was still there. Elvira had harbored a tiny hope that she had given up and gone on to Sulphur Springs without her.

"Thank the Lord!" she sobbed, clasping her hands to her huge bosom. "She's found—she's found! But what's the matter with her—she's not hurt, is she?

Oh Lord, I just knew that something terrible had happened . . ."

Mr. Lofton was carrying Elvira—she had said that she could walk just fine, but then she had wobbled so that he had insisted—and she was carrying the rosebush . . .

"No, ma'am, I don't believe she's hurt; she's just got a little temperature, that's all. Probably would be a good idea to have a doctor take a look at her."

Miss Ivy's face appeared behind Aunt Darla's. "Elvira, sweetheart—you're all right? Oh, thank goodness—you're all right!" She was crying, too . . .

And then Uncle Roy was there, and Roy Jr.—everyone but Hank—and there was a great deal of confusion and laughing and crying and hugging, while Mr. Lofton struggled to bring Elvira inside and put her on the couch . . . They all talked for a long time after that, or so it seemed to Elvira . . . and then Mr. Lofton said that he'd have to be going, and everyone had to thank him again and again and hear just once more the story of how he had found her . . . And then he was gone, and some redheaded policeman came by and asked a bunch of questions and smiled a lot, and then a doctor was there; Miss Ivy had gotten one to make a house call, somehow . . . He examined Elvira and told the women what ought to be done for her and left some medicine . . . and then they put her to bed and hugged her and cried over her some more . . .

They were getting ready to leave her to go to sleep when Elvira finally spoke; she had hardly said a word before now . . .

"Where's—where's my daddy?"

It was Miss Ivy who answered, in her gentle voice. "He's still out looking for you, sweetheart. He hasn't stopped looking since last night. You try to get some rest now, won't you? I'm sure he'll be home soon."

Hank was looking for her. He had never stopped looking for her . . . Miss Ivy closed the door. Elvira turned her face to her pillow and let the hot tears come. She was too tired to stop them.

She slept all the rest of that day and all that night and part of the next day, too. She dreamed a thousand dreams; they had been waiting for her on her pillow, it seemed . . . She dreamed of rain and roses and crawfish and cornstarch; she dreamed of doctors and ant beds and angels in heaven; she dreamed of Curtis and John David and roller coasters and catfish; and she dreamed of Hank . . . She dreamed that he was sitting beside her bed, stroking her hot head with his big, clumsy hand, straightening her covers, whispering soothing words when she cried out in her sleep . . .

And then she woke up, and he was there. It hadn't been a dream, after all. He had been right there, all along.

He had come home late Monday night, discouraged to death—ready to try again to cooperate with the police, ready to try anything that would bring his child back. And he had found her there.

When Elvira opened her eyes, he was dozing in a chair by the bed, with his cheek resting on his hand and his mouth hanging half open. He looked terrible—all scraggly and grungy . . . he needed a shave . . . he needed a shower. Elvira had never been so glad to see anybody in her life.

She sat up in bed and coughed a little—just a tiny cough, really; she didn't want to wake him—he looked so worn out. But he was awake in an instant, looking at her anxiously, feeling her forehead for any sign of fever . . . And then he saw that she was really awake now, too. His face changed; some of the anxiety left it and was replaced by the old Hank mask. He cleared his throat self-consciously.

"Well. You were pretty tired, huh?"

"Yessir, I guess so."

"You feelin' better?"

"Yessir, I feel just fine—I can get up now . . ."

"No, ma'am, you cain't. You still got a little fever. It's gone down a lot, but the doctor says you ought to stay in bed for at least a week, and I ain't takin' any chances . . . Not anymore," he added, under his breath.

That was a relief; Elvira sank back into her pillow. She really did feel better, but she was still weak as water . . . Her mind was moving slowly, like one of those super slo-mo's on the television baseball games . . . so slowly . . . It must be the medicine. She was quiet for a while; she just lay there, comfortably, listening to the small, unhurried sounds in the room—the ticking of the clock, the buzzing of a fly on the window screen, the creaking of Hank's chair, his slow, regular breathing—that was the best sound of all—the safest, best sound.

Her head felt empty—wonderfully empty—at rest . . . But, little by little, she began to have a feeling that there was something she had forgotten—something that had been worrying her that wasn't resolved yet . . . a great weight of worry that had lifted for a while, but was just waiting to fall again . . . She didn't really want to think of it, whatever it was, but somehow, she had to . . .

And then it all came back to her. The comfortable emptiness inside her head was suddenly filled with an enormous, snuffling presence. Elvira sighed.

"Is—is Aunt Darla still here?"

Hank nodded. "She says she won't leave until she's sure you're better."

Elvira sighed again. Of course Aunt Darla would wait; she wouldn't want to take a sick kid with her to Sulphur Springs—that might get germs all over her good car. If Aunt Darla hated sand so much, she probably wasn't a big germ fan, either . . .

"So—so I don't have to go right away, then? Till

I'm all the way well?" She swallowed hard; her throat was beginning to ache again.

Hank looked startled. "Go? You mean to Sulphur Springs?"

Elvira nodded slowly, wondering why he said it like that.

Hank rubbed his hand over his stubbly chin. "Well, sure—you wouldn't know . . . We talked about it so much I was thinkin' you knew, but acourse you were sleepin' . . . You don't hafta go nowhere, Elvira—nowhere you don't want to go."

The weight lifted once more; it disintegrated altogether. A slow, unbelieving joy began to take its place. Elvira sat up again; then she got up on her knees, put her hands on Hank's shoulders, and looked him straight in the eye. She had to be absolutely sure she had heard him right . . .

"I don't hafta go to Aunt Darla's—I can stay here with you?"

"As long as you want to, baby," said Hank in a choked voice. "Just as long as you want to . . ." And then he put his big old arms around her—kind of awkwardly, as if he didn't know exactly how to do it—and held her close. And for a good while after that, it would have been a lie to say that Aunt Darla was the only crybaby in the Trumbull family.

20

Elvira had a fine time being sick after that. Hank was as attentive as a fussy old mother hen; he was forever taking her temperature or fixing her soup—he branched out from tomato to chicken noodle—or bringing her soft drinks—Elvira had never had so much Coca-Cola in her entire life. They watched some television, too, but not all that much; Hank had somehow gotten it stuck in his head that it might strain her eyes, so he read to her, instead, just as if she were five years old again . . .

The rosebush was back in the garden. It was Hank who had replanted it, since he refused to budge an inch on the doctor's orders about keeping Elvira in bed. Every day he reported to her on its progress.

"Well, acourse, I don't know all that much about it, but it looks to me like it just might be all right . . ."

"You planted it like I told you, didn't you?" asked Elvira anxiously. "With the roots pointin' down and out? And you got to give it just the right amount of water . . ."

"I done it all just like you said, I swear," said Hank. "Don't you worry 'bout it, now. That rosebush'll prob'ly outlive all the rest of us put together." He grinned. "I just got an idea there's somethin' kinda hardheaded about it . . ."

Aunt Darla and her two male shadows came over faithfully every day until she had satisfied herself that Elvira really was on the mend and that Hank could be trusted to take care of her. To her credit, she seldom cried more than once a visit and never came without bringing two or three sacks full of groceries. Before her final departure for Sulphur Springs, the pantry and refrigerator and freezer of the little kitchen were bulging with so much stuff that Elvira decided it must be Aunt Darla's secret wish to get everybody else as fat as she was.

"I just hope there's a little meat on her bones the next time I see her," she told Hank on her last visit. "That child's always been too thin—she's frail, just like her mother was . . . Yogurt, that's what she needs. You give her a cupful of yogurt along with every meal, do you hear me? I intend to have a case of yogurt delivered here once a month; otherwise, I'll never get a wink of sleep at night—not that I do, anyway, what with Roy tossing and turning and getting up forty-seven times to go to the bathroom . . . Don't you roll your eyes at me, Roy Bledsoe—you know you do . . . Well, I suppose we ought to be running along, but it just breaks my heart to say good-bye; I had so counted on taking my little girl home with me . . . Just you remember, Ellie, if you ever change your mind—my house is your house . . ."

Elvira was hugely relieved when she was finally gone, but she found, to her surprise, that she no longer really hated Aunt Darla—now that she felt quite sure that she was never going to have to live with her. Aunt Darla wasn't such a terrible person, after all; she meant well—it probably wasn't really her fault that she had been born fat and obnoxious.

Miss Ivy came every day, too. At first, Elvira was a little shy of her; she couldn't quite forget the hurt of that rainy night. But Miss Ivy was so sweet and natural that it was impossible to feel strange around her for long. She made it quite clear that nothing had really changed, as far as she was concerned, and that she was still Elvira's good friend. She brought books and magazines and flowers from her garden, and, toward the end of the week, she brought Curtis and John David . . .

"We'll just stay for a little while," she explained. "I don't want them to tire you out, but they just had to see you with their own eyes and make sure you're really all right, didn't you, boys?"

Curtis looked serious. "You okay, Elvira?"

"Aw, sure, I'm just fine."

"Looka here—we brought you a present," said John David, handing her an oddly shaped package wrapped in old Christmas paper. "Curtis and me made it all by ourselfs."

"It's not too good," said Curtis, looking embarrassed, "but go on—open it . . ."

Elvira tore off the wrapping paper and lifted out a long-necked, hump-backed, yellow-and-red-spotted thingamajig.

"How 'bout that?" asked John David proudly.

"Well, it's real nice," said Elvira. "It's a real nice . . . uh . . . giraffe."

"You don't think it looks like a camel?" said Curtis.

"Not a bit—I mean, it's not s'posed to be a camel, is it?"

"No, it's a giraffe, all right," said John David. "See, Curtis—I told you it didn't look like a camel."

" 'Cept for that big hump on its back," muttered Curtis.

"Well, I think it's just fine," said Elvira. "It's the best giraffe I ever saw." She looked thoughtful. "I believe I'll name it Noreen . . ."

"We're gonna see a real giraffe in Hermann Park tomorrow," said John David happily. "Our daddy's not sick anymore, and we're gonna spend the weekend with him, and he's gonna take us to Astroworld and the zoo both."

"That's real nice," said Elvira. So their daddy really wasn't so bad, after all; Miss Ivy had been telling the truth about him. What was that she had said—no angels, no devils—just people . . .

And so the days passed, and Elvira got well. Summer ended, and school began. Hank found some part-time work pumping gas over at the filling station; when he had been there about a week, a woman brought in a station wagon that was spewing smoke and hissing like a snake. Nobody else at the station could do much with it, so Hank took a crack at it and had such good luck that the manager offered him a steady job as a mechanic. He took it.

The weather was especially fine that fall. The big

storm in August had spelled the end of the really awful heat; one bright, beautiful day was followed by another, and then another, even brighter and more beautiful. In Elvira's garden, the fall flowers were blooming; the marigolds and chrysanthemums and Gloriosa daisies were a blaze of gold and orange and red. And sure enough, there was a splash of pale yellow right in the middle, where the rosebush had managed one feeble little blossom. Just one scrawny flower, but it was a rose, all right—a real, live rose . . .

One cool evening in late October, Hank and Elvira were sitting in the kitchen having their supper when there was a knock at the front door.

"I'll get it," said Hank. He disappeared for a moment. When he came back, there was a puzzled expression on his face. He was holding a white envelope.

"That was the man from the office," he said. "He gave me this—said it had got mixed in with his mail, somehow . . ." Hank handed the envelope to Elvira. "It's for you."

"For me?" Elvira could hardly believe it; nobody had ever written her before. She tore it open. Two thin pieces of paper fluttered out. The first was a letter.

Dear Ms. Trumbull:

We at General Grains are sorry to hear of your dissatisfaction with our product. Please find enclosed a money order in the amount of $1.49. We hope that you will accept it with our apologies and that you will continue to be one of our valued customers.

Sincerely,
T. H. Hunter
Customer Relations

Elvira read it through once. She read it through again. Then she looked up at Hank and smiled a radiant smile. Wordlessly, she handed him the letter.

"Well, I'll swanny," he exclaimed softly, when he had read it. He smiled back at his daughter. "I'll swanny . . ."